"This one, I think."

Circe strode purposefully toward Harvey, who was still sitting, frozen, at the table across from Valerie.

"No!" Sabrina started toward Harvey.

Circe threw up an arm.

Instantly Sabrina felt as if she had run into an invisible brick wall. She stopped within an arm's reach of Harvey.

"Oh, yes," Circe said. "I believe this one is exactly the one I want." She gestured at Harvey.

Harvey shook his head, his eyelids fluttering as if he had just awakened. He stood up and looked around. Sabrina reached for him, thinking she could protect him if she could only touch him. "Harvey, come over here."

"No, Harvey," Circe ordered. "You'll be coming with me." She gestured and a silver chain suddenly appeared in her hand. The other end of it attached to a heavy brass collar that had appeared around Harvey's neck. "Remember your losses, little girl, and think twice before you offer disrespect to one who is your better."

Sabrina, the Teenage Witch™ books

#1 Sabrina, the Teenage Witch
#2 Showdown at the Mall
#3 Good Switch, Bad Switch
#4 Halloween Havoc
#5 Santa's Little Helper
#6 Ben There, Done That
#7 All You Need Is a Love Spell
#8 Salem on Trial
#9 A Dog's Life
#10 Lotsa Luck
#11 Prisoner of Cabin 13
#12 All That Glitters
#13 Go Fetch!
#14 Spying Eyes
Sabrina Goes to Rome
#15 Harvest Moon
#16 Now You See Her, Now You Don't
#17 Eight Spells a Week (Super Edition)
#18 I'll Zap Manhattan

Available from ARCHWAY Paperbacks

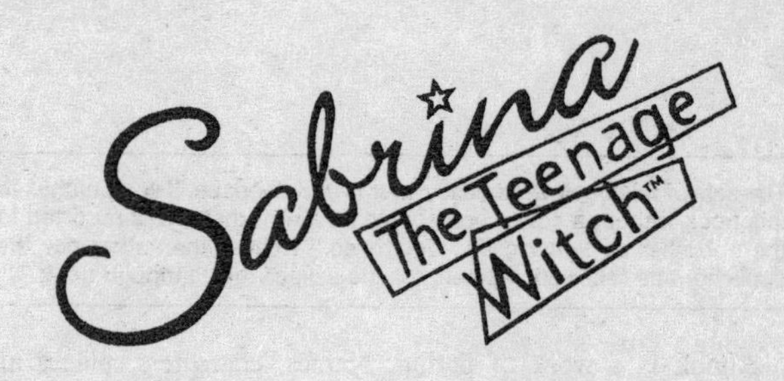

I'll Zap Manhattan

Mel Odom

Based on Characters Appearing in Archie Comics

And based upon the television series
Sabrina, The Teenage Witch
Created for television by Nell Scovell
Developed for television by Jonathan Schmock

AN ARCHWAY PAPERBACK
Published by POCKET BOOKS
New York London Toronto Sydney Tokyo Singapore

This book is a work of fiction. Names, characters, places and incidents are products of the author's imagination or are used fictitiously. Any resemblance to actual events or locales or persons living or dead is entirely coincidental.

AN ARCHWAY PAPERBACK *Original*

An Archway Paperback published by
POCKET BOOKS, a division of Simon & Schuster Inc.
1230 Avenue of the Americas, New York, NY 10020

ISBN: 0-671-02702-6

First Archway Paperback printing January 1999

10 9 8 7 6 5 4 3 2 1

Printed in the U.S.A.

IL: 4+

This book is dedicated with love from fathers to daughters for Valentine's Day.

To the charming Monya,
From her dad, Ethan Ellenberg

To the adorable and vocally gifted Alex,
From her dad, Phil Athans

To the enchanting Montana,
From her dad, Mel Odom

And to Lisa Clancy and Liz Shiflett, who believe in the good things

I'll Zap Manhattan

☆

Chapter 1

☆

Is there some unwritten rule that the really hot guys always catch you at your lamest? Sabrina Spellman blushed with embarrassment at being caught on her hands and knees peeking under the floral tablecloths covering the banquet tables in the formal dining room.

A black leather biker's jacket, a black turtleneck, black jeans, and silver-toed black boots sheathed the guy's lean, broad-shouldered frame. His dark curls ran wild, as challenging as the fire in his magnetic black eyes. But his smile shone open and genuine.

"I thought maybe I could help you look for whatever it is you lost." He extended a hand to help her up.

Electricity seemed to shoot through his fingers when he touched her hand, but he didn't appear to notice. Sabrina wore a lime green miniskirt with her hair pulled back in a braid. A little daring for the crowd around them, but she saw that he approved.

Dozens of people stood in the huge formal dining room. Most of them were conversing in small groups, and the constant buzz of voices created a background of noise. Spring bouquets decorated the tables. Back home in Westbridge, Massachusetts, in the mortal world, the bouquets would have been out of season and hard to come by. Here in the Other Realm, though, life could avoid the constraints of season or time.

Those constraints disappeared for the most part on Sabrina's sixteenth birthday. After being sent to live with her aunts, she had learned of her dual heritage—she was half witch and half mortal. Being a witch meant having really cool powers, even though it was a royal pain learning how to use them and getting licensed to practice them.

It also meant getting dragged to occasional witch functions like the one tonight. The evening's festivities centered on witches who'd made impressive contributions in the mortal realm—not using their spell-casting abilities. Sabrina's own aunt Zelda received honorable mention for her work in theoretical chemistry. Still, coming to the function meant breaking a Saturday night date with Harvey Kinkle at the Slicery back in Westbridge.

"So what did you lose?" he asked.

"My cat." Sabrina put her hands on her hips, broadcasting her irritation to Salem if he happened to be hiding somewhere and watching. "He's not easy to find if he doesn't want to be found."

"Creative tabby, huh?"

"Practically the Cheshire cat himself."

"I always liked *Alice in Wonderland,"* he said. "Especially the White Rabbit. When I was little, I trained for track events with him."

"You're kidding, right?"

"It's the truth. Mom book-sat me when she had things to do. Didn't your mom ever book-sit you?"

"No." *I had a perfectly normal childhood,* Sabrina thought. Well, maybe Let's Pretend to Explore King Tut's Tomb wasn't exactly every kid's dream of something to do, but her mortal archaeologist mom had been terrific. Especially when she occasionally gave in, after much pleading, and let Sabrina explore the mummy too. "My name's Sabrina Spellman. I'm half mortal. I was raised in the mortal world." *That sounded like a preamble for a dependency group.*

"Hey, that's cool!" A new smile, this one showing more teeth, spread across his face. "I'm Adam Vincent. It's nice to meet you."

"Likewise," Sabrina said. She felt kind of guilty standing there talking to him and feeling wowed by him with Valentine's Day less than a week away. And she still didn't have a gift for her boyfriend Harvey.

"About your cat," Adam said.

"His name's Salem," Sabrina told him.

Adam's eyebrows shot up. "Salem Saberhagen?"

"You've heard of him?"

"Oh, yeah. Are you kidding? Everybody's heard of the cat who tried to take over the world."

Actually, Salem hadn't been a cat at the time. He'd been a witch. The punishment of the Witches' Council had forced him to spend the next hundred years as a cat. Even as a cat, though, Salem often failed to walk the straight and narrow. His disappearance at the banquet was proof of that.

"Have you got a picture of him?" Adam asked.

Sabrina pointed a finger at her empty palm. Magic sparkles swirled, then a 35mm shot of Salem appeared. In his present incarnation, Salem was a black short-haired American cat.

"Terrific, we'll have him back in no time," Adam stated confidently. He pointed up a small glass sphere that spun at the end of his finger, reflecting light.

"A marble?" Sabrina asked.

"Not just any marble," Adam objected. "This is my Location Shooter. Of course, according to *The Discovery of Magic,* it can be anything glass or liquid that holds the spell. I just like using my shooter. Don't you have anything similar?"

"No. I guess I haven't gotten to that spell in the book yet." Actually, a lot of the book remained virtually unseen by Sabrina. She considered herself more of a hunt-and-peck witch, learning new spells as events or her education—or her aunts—required.

Adam pressed the marble shooter against the picture of Salem. He said two words in a language Sabrina didn't know. In the next instant the shooter rose from his hand and coasted through the air at a sedate pace. It floated over the ornately dressed tables toward a door at the back of the big room.

"Let's go," Adam urged, taking off at once.

The flashing marble spun through the air without hesitation. It shot past a guy standing with two African lions and past a woman who looked like an ancient gypsy dressed in a long sepia-colored dress. A large black crow shifted from foot to foot on her thin shoulder.

The marble zoomed along the wall at the end of the room, zipping around the small groups. Sabrina ducked under a woman's hat to follow Adam, barely avoiding the leathery bat wings that stuck out nearly two feet on either side of her head.

The marble paused at a closed doorway leading to another room off the formal dining room. Adam cautiously opened the door. Darkness filled the next room. Dust covered the floor. It was so big Sabrina couldn't see the other end.

"Guess they don't use this room much," Sabrina said. She felt a little creeped out. Empty and unused rooms in the Other Realm often turned out to be places to avoid.

"No," Adam agreed. He snapped his fingers and a flaming torch appeared in his hand while an Indiana Jones fedora dropped onto his head. He adjusted the headgear. "My lucky hat. I don't go into any strange, dark place in the Other Realm without it."

Sabrina reluctantly followed him into the space that was more cavern than room. She had thought the formal dining room was huge, but this room was even bigger. The ceiling stood at least ten feet taller. Buildings, when the witches bothered with them at all, didn't always follow mortal designs or expectations.

"Must be an amphitheater of some sort," Adam said.

Before Sabrina could reply, a loud growling snarl echoed inside the room. She grabbed Adam's arm, thinking instantly of the lions in the other room.

The marble shot forward into the darkness, then hovered in place just beyond the glow of Adam's torch.

Sabrina recognized the noise when it was repeated. She stepped out from behind Adam. "Salem," she called.

"Sabrina?" The cat blinked in pain, his eyes glowing in the torchlight. He lay stretched out in the remains of several platters.

"What are you doing here?" Sabrina demanded. The growls hadn't been those of a monster; they'd been Salem in the throes of indigestion. She'd seen him that way before. "If you ate all of this rich food, you should be in misery."

"I am, I am," Salem groaned. "Can't I have the guilt later? Please zap me up an antacid for now." He moaned again and made plaintive crying sounds.

Despite the fact that Salem's appetite had gotten him into trouble, Sabrina felt sorry for the cat. She pointed up a liquid antacid in a dish, then put it in front of Salem.

The cat's pink tongue darted out to lap at it. Almost immediately the angry growling from his stomach stopped. "Oh, that's so much better." He curled back up on the floor.

"How did you get all that food in here?" Sabrina asked. Not having hands was one of the reasons the Witches' Council had chosen a cat's body for Salem.

"I talked Finestral's familiar into it," Salem answered.

"I don't know either one of them," Sabrina said.

"You can't miss them," Adam volunteered. "Finestral wears a stovepipe hat and a neon-light-studded jacket. His familiar, Handel, is a minisquid living in a wheeled mop bucket."

Sabrina recalled the duo easily, though she hadn't been introduced. By choice. Shaking hands with a squid, even a small one, didn't sound pleasant.

"Handel's a good guy, once you get past all those arms," Salem admitted.

"I'll take your word for it." Suddenly interested in the possibilities offered by the room, Sabrina turned and peered into the darkness. "You know, with a little magic, this room could turn out to be a great place to dance."

"Plenty of room," Adam agreed. "And I don't think anyone would mind if we used it."

"Oh, come on," Salem groaned. "There's something to be said for peace and quiet."

"Yes," Sabrina agreed. "There's been way too much of it tonight." She looked at Adam. "Follow my lead?"

"Sure."

Sabrina focused her thoughts, finding all the rhymes she needed to make the spell work.

"Room that's dark and full of gloom,
now be clean by mop and broom."

Instantly, a whole brigade of brooms whisked across the floor in military ranks, followed closely by mops.

She continued:

"Room that has no kites,
now be filled with party lights."

"No kites?" Adam echoed.

"It rhymes," Sabrina said defensively.

The walls shimmered, then the darkness draping the room disappeared as lights zapped into place on the walls and ceiling. Sabrina kept zapping up new lighting arrangements, and Adam added a few.

In minutes the big room looked fantastic, brightly lighted and festooned with wall graffiti in neon colors. All of the drawings were of dancers.

"Are you about done with the dance floor?" Adam asked.

"Just a minute," Sabrina said. To add more dance floor, she zapped up a catwalk that ran around three sides of the room. *Maybe I'm being ambitious, but I think MTV would feel at home here.*

"That looks great," Adam told her. "Now we need a sound, something that's going to appeal to a lot of people."

"Fifties' and sixties' music then," Sabrina said.

Adam smiled, snapping his fingers and creating a pair of wraparound black sunglasses and a ten-foot surfboard. "There can be only one choice then."

"The remaining Beach Boys," Sabrina agreed, feeling the rush of excitement fill her.

Adam flipped the surfboard out and it hung in the air three feet above the ground. He stepped up on to it, then reached back for Sabrina.

She managed the step up with his help. Surprisingly, the broad surfboard had a lot of room to dance. "This flies?" It bobbed only slightly beneath their combined weight as they moved.

"Beats a broom, don't you think?" Adam asked. "What do you fly?"

"Uh, a vacuum cleaner," Sabrina admitted.

"That's"—Adam paused, one of his cute smiles not fitting exactly right—"very traditional of you."

Sabrina gestured, setting the overhead lights into motion. She spotted a few curious people poking their heads in through the door. "It's showtime," she told Adam.

Adam gave a quick nod, then his voice took on a new timbre:

"Rock 'n' roll, fill my cup.
Give us the Beach Boys, 'cause *Surf's Up!*"

A powerful wind whipped through the room, and lightning flicked a jagged tongue from one end to the other. It touched down and in the blink of an eye created a stage against the empty fourth wall.

White smoke boiled from the stage, and bright pink, yellow, green, and blue laser beams shot across the room, rebounding from the light systems Sabrina had zapped up.

"Cool," Sabrina said delightedly.

The musicians hesitated for only a moment after appearing, then launched into one of their all-time fave hits. The rock 'n' roll music blared to life in full Surround Sound.

"Well," Sabrina said, speaking loud enough for Adam to hear above the roar of the music, "here's where we find out if we're grounded for the next month for interrupting a serious occasion."

The music continued to build as the lead singer danced around the stage. The drummer tossed him a wireless headset and he put it on. His mellow baritone pealed through the room. "So how 'bout it, people? Feel like surfin'?"

Immediately the witches poured in from the banquet room and claimed dancing space. In seconds the once-empty room had become a party bursting at the seams as the Beach Boys rock 'n' rolled the boredom away.

"I'd say we're a hit," Adam shouted.

Sabrina nodded, giving herself over to the music and making use of the surfboard's surface. It felt good to be moving.

"Hang on," Adam suggested. He pointed at the surfboard and flickering running lights strobed into being. He pointed up a lei for himself and one for Sabrina, and even added one for Salem, who had joined them and didn't seem overly appreciative. Adam then zapped up dozens more. He flew the surfboard around the room and tossed the leis out to the dancers.

"We have just become Party Central," Sabrina bragged.

"Oh, yeah," Adam agreed. "This is one theoretical science banquet that will never be the same."

"Sabrina! Sabrina!"

Recognizing her aunt Hilda's voice, Sabrina glanced down into the crowd.

Hilda was there, cupping her hands to be heard above the noise. She wore a short skirt and a sleeveless shirt with a gaudy parrot print. Fun-loving as always, she had evidently been one of the first to join in. "Great party!" she called, then flashed a thumbs-up sign.

Sabrina noticed that Hilda was dancing with Drell, the witch she had been chasing for hundreds of years. Drell had gotten into the spirit of the party, dressed in an obnoxious Hawaiian shirt and tan baggies. "Thanks," she called back.

By the time they'd thrown out all the leis, Sabrina guessed that nearly all of the banquet-goers had funneled into the party. Even Zelda seemed to be having a good time.

Sabrina and Adam danced on the lighted surfboard as it floated over the heads of the partygoers. Adam even made the surfboard do barrel rolls, keeping them on it with his magic. Sabrina waved her hands above her head, getting totally wild and loving it. Salem, though, held his paws over his mouth and made threats about getting sick.

Suddenly a serious blast of lightning and thunder swelled through the room.

"Oh man," Adam groaned, looking over Sabrina's shoulder. "Trouble!"

☆

Chapter 2

☆

Sabrina stared at the girl Adam had referred to as trouble.

The girl looked elfin and elegant standing in the doorway from the banquet room. Close-cropped dark hair pulled back from a face filled with unearthly beauty. Makeup brought out the luster of her purple eyes beneath the delicate arched brows. Full lips the color of cherries formed a pout. A silk camisole clung to her body like a second layer of skin, the color an absolute match for the purple of her eyes. The top was tucked into black leggings that were in turn tucked into knee-high black leather boots.

Everyone in the room stopped dancing to stare at the new arrival. Even the musicians seemed stunned to see her.

"Who is she?" Sabrina asked.

"Her name is Circe."

"Like the witch in *The Odyssey?*"

"She *was* the witch in *The Odyssey,*" Adam replied.

"Check out the guys in the monkey suits," Salem suggested.

For the first time Sabrina noticed the four men surrounding Circe. They were all squat and broad, like professional football linemen. And they were each covered with hair, their faces not really even human.

"Those aren't suits," Sabrina gasped. "Those are real apes!"

Adam nodded. "Guy-rillas, actually. Maybe they were men once, but it was so long ago they probably don't remember. Now they serve Circe."

Sabrina couldn't believe what she was hearing. Things were done differently in the Other Realm. She'd kind of gotten adjusted to that. Even Hilda had turned a few guys into toads for being jerks over the years. She always turned them back . . . eventually.

"Nobody told me there'd be a party after the banquet," Circe announced in regal tones. She used magic to make her voice loud enough to be heard by everyone. "I almost missed it." She walked on into the room, which suddenly started to change shape.

A wide stairwell that hadn't been there an eye blink before suddenly unfurled and corkscrewed down to the dance floor from a doorway high overhead. Circe dragged her fingers along the polished wood of the banister. Two of the guy-rillas walked in front of her while the other two trailed behind.

"But maybe I should say," Circe told them, "that *you* almost missed it. This band is pretty lame." She pointed and blasted the entire band off the stage in a cloud of roiling black smoke.

"Are they okay?" Sabrina asked Adam.

He nodded after a second. "They're fine. Back in their hotel rooms. They won't remember this."

"Why isn't someone doing something?"

"Sabrina," Adam said quietly, "you don't know how powerful Circe is. Usually the best approach to handle her is to let her have her way. She gets bored pretty quickly and moves on."

Sabrina watched the woman as she continued down the impossibly long staircase. "What's she even doing here?"

"Circe's the top authority on pocket dimensions in the realms," Adam said. "My dad came out here just to listen to the panel she was on."

"Pocket dimensions?"

Adam nodded. "Some of the Ancients have learned how to create their own worlds within the realms. Circe has her own world."

"Then why leave it?" Sabrina pictured an immense palace filled with guy-rillas who attended Circe's every need. It wasn't exactly her idea of paradise.

"They get bored. No matter how well thought out their worlds are, there's nothing like interaction with others."

Circe's voice rose again. "If you wanted to party, you should have let me know. No one loves a good party as much as I do." She reached the bottom of the stairs and strode out onto the stage area. It was even bigger than Sabrina had designed.

Sabrina peered out over the crowd. Some of the witches started to slip away, but the only exit was up the tall staircase. She couldn't see Zelda or Hilda anywhere.

Circe worked her magic effortlessly, pointing up an orchestra on the left side of the stage, followed by a group of backup singers on the right. The orchestra was complete with strings, brass, and woodwind instruments. The backup singers were all beautiful women in shimmering gowns that looked as if they were covered with rainbow-colored fish scales.

The band played a muscled version of a popular Motown hit from the sixties. And the backup singers crooned a harmony that was hypnotic, their voices like nothing Sabrina had ever heard.

As Circe walked across the stage, her clothing changed into a long flowing red dress that accentuated her hair and complexion and flaunted her perfect figure. She held out an empty hand, then wrapped it around the microphone one of the guy-rillas handed her.

Sabrina felt angry as she watched Circe start strutting across the stage, opening herself up to the rhythm of the song. The witch had no right to crash Sabrina's party the way she had. She schemed, wondering how best to save the situation.

"You've got that look in your eye," Salem said plaintively at her feet. "Now isn't the time to do anything foolish."

"So we should just let her crash our party?" Sabrina asked.

"In a word, yes," Salem said. "It would be the safest thing to do."

"Salem's right," Adam told her. "Going head-to-head with Circe is strictly a bad idea."

"Unless you think you'd look good in a fur coat," Salem said.

"No," Sabrina admitted, her mind furiously engaged. "But this was our party. I'm not going to let her get away with this. I've got an idea. Coming?"

Adam was hesitant. "Sabrina, really, bucking Circe isn't a good idea. We could hang out here, listen to a few songs—"

"You can do that if you want. I'm not." Sabrina started to step off the surfboard.

"Wait," Adam said, "I'll go with you. Where to?"

"The next room."

"There's not another room except for the banquet area."

"There is now," Sabrina corrected, pointing at the door she zapped into being on the wall opposite the stage.

Adam guided the surfboard through the door and into the room beyond. It was warehouse-huge and empty. "So what's the plan?"

"Battle of the Bands," Sabrina replied, zapping up a stage and decorations hurriedly.

"What band?" Adam asked.

"*The* band," Sabrina answered, smiling. "The Fab Four."

"Uh, did you know there are currently only three of them left?"

"No problemo," Sabrina said. "I'm going to bring their past selves to the party, not their present selves." As a present for Aunt Hilda's last birthday, she had crafted a special spell that allowed her to travel back in time with Hilda to the early days of the band in England. All she had to do now was use a variation on that same spell to bring the group here.

"Bring me the singers, bring me the band,
I gotta have the group that wants to hold
my hand."

She pointed at the stage, feeling all of the pent-up magic spewing from her finger.

With a loud *bamf!* the singers dropped onto the stage, complete with instruments. One of them stepped forward to the end of the stage. He looked so young and handsome in his dark suit. "Sabrina," he called out in his English accent, "is that you, love?"

"Yes. I was wondering if you'd mind doing me a favor," Sabrina said. She had gotten to meet the group when she'd taken Hilda to see them.

He looked at the other three players, then looked back at Sabrina. "Well, love, I guess we are here after all. What's going on?"

Quickly, over the roar of Circe's band, Sabrina explained the situation.

"You know what?" the singer said with a small, mischievous smile when Sabrina finished. "It sounds like you've had a hard day's night." Then he turned back to the others and started singing.

With the acoustics and the speaker system Sabrina had zapped up, the song rolled out to fill the room.

Almost instantly, the witches began trickling into the room Sabrina had zapped up. By the time the band launched into a spirited rendition of "Long, Tall Sally," Sabrina doubted that anyone remained in the other room.

Sure enough, the music in the other room died out. Dancing on the floating surfboard with Adam, Sabrina couldn't help but smile. She'd won. She looked out into the crowd, hoping to spot Hilda or Zelda, but neither of them appeared to be around.

Finished with the latest song, the singer called out, "Hey, Sabrina, we thought you might like to help us out with this one."

"No," Sabrina said, "I couldn't." The audience roared their approval, a few of them calling out Sabrina's name. The sound was music to Sabrina's ears. *Okay, maybe I can.*

Salem wagged his head sorrowfully. "I really don't like the look of this crowd."

"What if I don't know the words?" Sabrina asked, descending from the surfboard to the stage, and suddenly realizing she might not be up to this.

"If you don't know this one," the singer said, "we're not doing this right." He cued the band.

As soon as the song started, Sabrina relaxed. It was a fave of hers, "Twist and Shout," and she *did* know all the words. Even though she knew she was not a good singer, Sabrina surprised herself by really cutting loose and putting her heart and soul into the performance. Thoughts of not having Harvey's Valentine's Day gift and the last few boring hours of the banquet were a million miles away.

But just as the song faded, a harsh clangor filled the air.

Spotlights flashed on a second stage that had been zapped into the room at the other end. Circe, dressed in torn jeans with the knees out, a baby blue halter top under a black leather jacket, and assorted body piercings through her lips and eyebrows, flipped up on stage with the grace of a trained acrobat. Her makeup had changed, too. Garish greens and purples warred, making her eyes look huge and malicious.

Circe screamed in primal rage, than started shouting the lyrics of the song as the band did their best to blow out the amps and speakers. Most of the witches didn't make it past the guy-rilla's drum solo. Suspended above the floor, the drumset whirled over and over while the guy-rilla banged away. Before he righted himself and the song started up again, nearly all of the witches had zapped themselves back home or someplace else.

"Party's over," Salem said as Adam flew the surfboard over to pick up Sabrina. "Time to go home while I'm the only one wearing the fur around here."

Circe finished her song and stood panting on the other stage, glaring at Sabrina. She didn't seem to notice the absence of an audience, too blinded by the spotlights to see. She tossed her microphone aside. It landed with a resounding thump on the stage because it was still switched on. She jumped from the stage and marched toward Sabrina.

Moving quickly, the teenage witch zapped the band back in time and hopped aboard Adam's surfboard. He flew them toward the door fast enough to create a breeze.

It wasn't fast enough, though. An iron-barred gate appeared across the door.

Adam barely got the surfboard stopped in time, sending all three of them tumbling to the floor. Salem was the only one who landed on his feet.

Sabrina got up quickly, watching helplessly as Circe approached her. The four guy-rillas trailed closely behind her, their lips pulled back, revealing huge fangs.

Circe stopped inches in front of Sabrina. "Who are you, little girl?" the ancient witch demanded.

"Sabrina Spellman."

"Have you any idea who you're trifling with?" Circe asked.

"I know your name," Sabrina replied. "And I also know you're selfish and rude. You've crashed *two* parties."

"I tried to save both pathetic excuses you had for parties, you mean."

"I forgot to add conceited," Sabrina admitted. She tried to zap herself, Adam, and Salem out of the room, but she felt only a weak fizzle in her finger. She couldn't just point her way out of the current mess.

"You're going to be sorry you shoved your nose into my business, girl." Circe drew a hand back, preparing to let fly with a spell as the guy-rillas surrounded them.

Sabrina braced herself, knowing there was no way she could stand up to Circe's magic. She tried to decide what animal she'd least like to become and was surprised by how many there were. Looking at the guy-rillas, she really hoped they weren't animals that ate their own fleas.

☆

Chapter 3

☆

"No!"

At first Sabrina thought the hoarse scream came from herself. Then she realized she was holding her breath and had her eyes closed as well. She opened them, relieved to see she still had her own body.

Circe faced away from her, watching Hilda and Zelda approach. Drell followed closely and reluctantly behind the two. "Who are you?" Circe demanded. She kept her finger poised threateningly.

Zelda remained composed as she faced Circe. "I'm Sabrina's aunt and a representative of the Witches' Council. I'm sure you know Drell."

"I know Drell," Circe admitted. "But I don't know what you're doing here."

"Stopping you from making a big mistake," Hilda added.

Circe made a point of scrutinizing Hilda, then obviously grimaced in distaste. "Another aunt," she said in her accent. "The family oafishness is easily detected."

Hilda's dimples deepened and her face colored in anger. Lightning flashed across the ceiling and thunder rolled like cannonshot. "How would you like to spend the next decade in an iron maiden at the bottom of the Pacific Ocean?"

"You aren't witch enough to put me there," Circe said.

"No," Zelda agreed in a barely calm voice, "but the Witches' Council is. Your behavior tonight hasn't gone unnoticed. If you touch one hair on Sabrina's head, you're going to regret it."

Sabrina had never seen her aunt so scary or so angry. Zelda was usually the epitome of cool.

Circe gestured at herself, zapping away the punk rocker getup and going back to her original clothing. "This child needs reprimanding. She dared thwart me and interrupt my pleasures. She shall pay dearly for that. A few decades as a goat will teach her humility and respect for her elders."

"What?" Sabrina exploded. *A goat? No way am I going to be turned into a goat. They have beards, horns, and those floppy ears. How would that look in a yearbook?*

"Maybe if her elders looked more like her elders," Hilda suggested, "instead of high-school cheerleaders, it would help."

Circe glared at Hilda. "Not all of us have to look middle-aged."

"You're not turning Sabrina into a goat," Zelda said.

"Do you propose to stop me?" Circe lifted one thin, arched brow. Her hand was raised threateningly.

Hilda nudged Drell hard enough to make him take a step forward.

"Actually," Drell put in, sticking a finger into the collar of his shirt and pulling it loose, "the Witches' Council is going to stop you."

Circe took a step toward Drell, who towered over her. She traced his nose with one wickedly pointed fingernail. "Is that right, Drell? Will they stop me?"

"Yes." In Sabrina's opinion, Drell's voice lacked a little in commitment.

The four guy-rillas leaned in, surrounding Hilda, Zelda, Drell, Salem, Adam, and Sabrina. Their close-set eyes showed only hostility over their flaring nostrils.

"Well, we'll just have to see about that," Circe threatened. She turned to face Sabrina again. "It appears, little girl, that you've escaped my wrath—for the moment."

"Wrath?" Salem made loud guffawing noises as he walked to the end of Adam's floating surfboard. "Who writes your dialogue, lady? A straight-to-video hack?" He sat at the end of the surfboard and cocked his head to one side as he curled his tail around his paws.

Over Circe's shoulder, Sabrina saw expressions of horror on her aunts' faces. They shook their heads, trying desperately to shush the cat. She knew at once that whatever protection the Witches' Council had over her did not cover Salem.

Understanding the expressions, Salem suddenly sat up, his ears straight, his mouth a frightened *O* of surprise. "Did I say that out loud?"

"You're a brave little kitty," Circe purred. "But you don't have to remain either of those: brave or a kitty. You might keep that in mind."

Sabrina reached down and picked up Salem, cradling him with her body.

Circe regarded her with fiery anger. "Another time, Sabrina Spellman. Another place. I don't suffer fools or impertinence gladly." She waved a hand and zapped herself out of the room, taking the entourage of guy-rillas with her.

"Wow," Adam said with genuine relief, "that was close."

Drell mopped his forehead with a handkerchief. "I must admit, Sabrina, taking on an Ancient isn't a sign of intelligence."

"I didn't do anything to her," Sabrina objected. "We started a party to break up the postbanquet boredom. Not everyone felt like standing around talking about quarks and tachyons and event horizons." She looked at Zelda. "I don't mean to hurt your feelings. I think it's great that you get a chance to talk with your friends."

Zelda sighed. "You're right, of course. There's only so much food a person can eat—no matter how good it is. I know none of us anticipated how long we'd stand around talking, but it's so seldom we all get to be together."

"And," Drell said, "you knew that inviting Circe would probably lead to trouble. But you insisted on inviting her anyway."

"It would have been even worse if we hadn't invited her," Zelda pointed out.

"That's true," Hilda put in. "You know how she can get. Remember Pompeii? The research board didn't invite her that year, either, and look at what happened there when that volcano erupted."

"I don't think you've seen the last of her," Adam stated. "Circe tends to hold a grudge."

"I know," Zelda said, "that's why the Witches' Council gave us this." She held out an open palm. Immediately a bracelet made of twisted copper wire intertwined with small red and green leaves appeared.

"What's that?" Sabrina asked.

"A bracelet of protection. It should keep

Circe's magic from working on you as long as you wear it."

"I have to wear that—that—" Sabrina stared at the twisted wire-and-leaf bracelet, not believing what she was hearing. "But I don't have a thing that I can wear with it."

"Zap something up."

"What? Tree bark? Barbed wire? I don't think that bracelet would work if I went totally punk *or* Goth."

Salem looked up at her and bleated like a goat. "Maaaaa. Maaaa. Maaaaaaaaa."

"Oh, yeah. Right." Sabrina stuck out her arm. The twisted metal felt cool against Sabrina's skin. And heavy. She moved her arm experimentally, not liking the feel of the bracelet at all. "How long do I have to wear this?"

Her aunts looked at each other.

"Well," Hilda said, "Circe has been known to hold grudges for a long time."

"How long is a long time?" Sabrina asked.

Hilda made a face, obviously not wanting to talk about it. Zelda maintained her silence.

Sabrina lifted the bracelet and smelled it. "It stinks. I can't go to school with this on my arm."

"Maybe," Salem put in, "it would be easier to go to school as Billy Goat Gruff."

"I'm afraid you're stuck with it," Hilda said.

"At least until we can figure out what to do about Circe," Zelda said.

"What?" Sabrina asked.

Zelda shook her head. "I honestly don't know yet. We were lucky we could get enough of the Witches' Council together to get this bracelet made. It's not easy binding an Ancient, and Circe is one of our most ancient members. There's a lot we don't know about them."

Sabrina twisted the smelly bracelet on her wrist, dreading the whole thought of wearing it to school.

"We need to be getting home," Hilda said. "I think we've had enough excitement for one night."

Sabrina silently agreed, quickly said good-bye to Adam and Drell, and thanked Drell for his help. Then Zelda zapped them all back to the linen closet in the Spellman house.

Back in the mortal realm, it was only eight forty-five. Time flowed differently in different realms, and even though hours of the evening had been spent at the banquet, there were hours left in Sabrina's day at home. It didn't, however, make her any less tired.

Her immediate attention turned to Circe. She wanted to talk to her aunts about the ancient witch, but they wanted to do some networking to find out the latest rumors about the woman.

Wanting to relax, Sabrina took a bath the old-fashioned way instead of just zapping herself clean. She even splurged on bath-oil beads, creating a heady fragrance in the steamy water.

But it wasn't enough to take her mind off her current situation. For one thing the leafy bracelet smelled even worse when it got wet.

Back in her room in her PJs and robe, she threw herself on her bed. A lightning swift coil of black fur, Salem, leaped up and joined her. She could smell tuna on his breath even over the stench of the protective bracelet.

"You've been eating again?" she asked in disbelief.

"Hey," Salem said defensively, "we all worry in our own way. Hilda and Zelda gossip, you bathe, and I eat."

Sabrina zapped up a kitty-treat breath mint.

Salem pushed a paw at it, moving it away. "No, really, I couldn't eat another bite."

"Eat this or go in the other room."

He looked up at her. "That bad, huh?"

"Yes."

"I never have understood how tuna can taste so good and smell so bad. Is it as bad as that bracelet?"

Sabrina glared at him.

"Touchy, aren't we?"

"Eat the mint."

Salem flipped the mint up into the air with his nose, then caught it expertly in his teeth on the way back down. He made a show of chewing and swallowing. "So, what are we going to do about the Wicked Witch of the Beast?"

"I don't know, but I'm going to have to do

something. Wearing this smelly bracelet is *not* an option." She sat up on her bed and zapped *The Discovery of Magic* book over to her. It floated slowly. Once it was open across her knees, she touched the cover and zapped again.

The book opened to the beginning of the section on Circe. Sabrina had expected a monograph on the Ancient and maybe links to a few other entries. What she hadn't expected were the pages and pages and pages that had been written on Circe.

"Oh wow," Sabrina gasped. Besides the text, there were a lot of pictures too. "I didn't know there was so much about her." She leafed through the pages.

"The scary thing is that it's still not enough."

Sabrina scanned the pages. As she read, the idea of wearing the bracelet didn't seem quite so bad. In fact, she started to wonder if it might not need to be bigger and smellier.

Some of the information she knew she had heard in a lit class when they read Homer's *Odyssey,* but it had lasted only until the test covering that section.

Circe's parents consisted of Perse, who was a daughter of a Greek ocean god, and Helios, the sun god. She had a brother named Aaetes and a stepsister named Aega.

After nearly an hour of reading, though, all Sabrina really got was sleepy. She tried lying in different positions, even sitting at the desk in her room, but nothing worked. Her eyelids finally got too heavy to keep open.

"Sabrina."

The harsh whisper woke Sabrina instantly. She opened her eyes to darkness in the room. Someone had visited the room long enough to turn the lights out and throw an afghan over her. She felt warm despite the winter chill frosting the windowpanes.

"Over here, little girl."

Sabrina recognized the voice even though it was whispering. "Circe?"

"Come closer," the ancient witch called.

Drawn by the taunting lilt of Circe's voice, Sabrina got up from her bed and approached the full-length mirror in the corner of the room. She watched the shadow moving in the shallow depths beneath her own reflection. Cold fear pricked her skin, reminding her of the childhood game she used to play. *Bloody Mary,* she thought.

The dark shadow of Circe stirred beneath Sabrina's reflection. An evil grin twisted the face. "I wanted to let you know that I know you, little girl. I know who you are, I know where you live, and I know what you think. I can reach out and touch you anytime I want." She lifted her shadow hand and pushed it through Sabrina's reflection, reaching through the glass.

The arm moved through the mirror up to the elbow, causing Sabrina to step backward. The arm glistened as if it were constructed of liquid rather than flesh and bone.

"Afraid, Sabrina?" Circe's mocking laughter followed her hand through the glass.

Angry, Sabrina swept her bracelet toward the shadowy arm. When the leafy metal braid touched the hand, the hand evaporated. "You can't touch me," Sabrina said.

Inside the mirror the shadowy Circe was whole again. "I will, though, little girl. I'll take that which you care about most. Then we'll see how untouched you are."

Before Sabrina could speak, the shadow Circe gestured at Sabrina's reflection. In the next instant, Sabrina's mirror image crystallized and exploded, the pieces rebounding from the mirror's surface, then winking out like sparks.

Circe's shadow was gone, and the mirror remained empty, reflecting only the room behind Sabrina. Letting out a tense breath, she recited a quick spell:

"Mirror that makes my image's map,
now be covered with pleasant wrap."

Immediately brilliant Christmas wrap covered the full-length mirror. A big green bow held it all together.

"Sabrina?"

Starting at the voice, Sabrina turned around to see Salem slinking into the room. "Oh, it's you."

The cat sat on his haunches and stared up at her. "Is something wrong?"

"Yes." Quickly, Sabrina related the events that had just happened.

"You need to tell Zelda and Hilda," Salem said when she finished.

"I will," Sabrina declared. "But in the morning, okay? I know they're probably tired too." She glanced at the mirror. "But I'm not staying here tonight." She picked up a pillow.

"Want company?" Salem asked.

"Sure." She zapped them both down to the living room and onto the couch. For the first few minutes, she lay there and quietly tried to go to sleep.

Salem stretched himself across the top of the couch. "Get some sleep."

"I don't know if I can." Every time Sabrina closed her eyes, she saw Circe's hand reaching for her through the mirror.

Salem stroked her hair with a paw. "Sure you can. Just close your eyes and remember that I've got your back."

Finally managing to find a comfortable position on the couch, Sabrina drifted off to sleep.

☆

Chapter 4

☆

"Are you up, Sabrina?" Hilda called from the kitchen.

Struggling to free herself from the afghan and her twisted PJs, Sabrina called back, "I am now." She briefly considered zapping herself into her school clothes, but decided against it. She felt miserable, and the only way to reap any enjoyment out of the feeling was to wallow in it.

"Come into the kitchen and I'll zap you up a cup of hot cocoa," Zelda offered.

As soon as Sabrina's feet touched the cold wooden floor, she yanked them up again and yelped in surprise.

Instantly, Zelda and Hilda zapped themselves into the room. Both had their pointing fingers at the ready.

"What is it?" Hilda asked.

"Cold floor," Sabrina said apologetically.

Hilda zapped a pair of grape-colored bunny slippers onto Sabrina's feet. The lop ears flopped to the sides. "Come into the kitchen and we'll get you warmed up."

Looking around the room, Sabrina suddenly noticed that Salem was missing. She remembered Circe's promise to take something from her. "Where's Salem?"

"It's okay," Zelda said. "Salem's in the kitchen eating breakfast."

"He told us about last night's visitor," Hilda said.

Sabrina sat at the table and Zelda zapped up a cup of hot cocoa topped with whipped cream. Both the aunts had coffee. Neither of them, Sabrina noticed, looked particularly rested.

"You should have woken us," Zelda said across from Sabrina.

"You guys were tired," Sabrina said. "Anyway, what could you have done?"

"We could have put up protective wards around the house," Hilda said. "The way we did this morning after Salem told us about last night. We also talked with your father this morning and he's taking care of himself. As for your mother, he helped me ward the dig site she's on in Peru."

Sabrina nodded glumly.

"Do you feel like going to school today?"

Hilda asked. "If you don't, we can call the school secretary and clear your absence."

"I want to go to school," Sabrina said. "Maybe not to class, but I don't plan on becoming a hermit in my room."

"We know how you feel," Zelda said. "But it might be for the best."

"Would you want to be trapped in your own house?"

"No," Zelda said without hesitation. Hilda agreed.

"The thing that Circe could take away from me that I care about the most is my life," Sabrina said. "I can't let her disrupt my schedule."

"Discretion has always been the better part of valor," Salem advised from the countertop.

Sabrina held up the bracelet. "I've got this. She can't do anything to me as long as I'm wearing it, right?"

Zelda hesitated. "Technically."

"Nobody told me there were going to be technicalities about wearing this."

"What Zelda means," Hilda said, "is that as far as we know Circe has no power over you while you're wearing the bracelet. But we don't know for certain how long the protection is going to last."

"But that could happen even if I stayed home."

"However," Hilda said, "we do have extra wards around the house now. We can't put them around the school because it's a public place."

"But I'm only a zap away from home," Sabrina said. "If Circe shows up at school, I'll just zap home."

The aunts swapped doubtful looks.

Sabrina took a deep breath, marshaling her final argument. "If I stay here, I won't stop worrying. And I'll go absolutely bonkers. Maybe I'll take you with me."

"She does have a point," Hilda said.

Zelda nodded. "Okay, but we're going to ward you so that we know the instant anything magical happens to you."

"Do you really think that's necessary?" Sabrina had visions of herself walking around Westbridge High with an antimagic CLUB strapped to her body. The bracelet was going to be hard enough to explain.

"Yes," Zelda said, "we think it's necessary." She pointed at Sabrina's neck.

A blossom of colored sparkles coiled around Sabrina's neck.

"Here," Zelda said, pointing up a hand mirror that floated in front of Sabrina.

Looking into the reflection brought up thoughts of Circe. Sabrina quickly checked the depths for any shadowy beings but saw only her reflection. A tiny crystal heart with a gold arrow encased within it hung from a white gold necklace in the hollow of her throat. Closer inspection revealed the ruby arrowhead on the gold shaft.

"This is beautiful," Sabrina exclaimed, touching the small crystal heart with her fingertips. Instead of being smooth, it had several facets that caught and splintered the light.

"Besides being beautiful," Zelda said, "it also comes with a warning system. If you come within a few feet of a magic item, spell, or another witch, the pendant will signal Hilda and me. All we have to do is peer into the nearest reflective surface to see you."

"And it makes a great early Valentine's Day present," Hilda said.

"It's a good idea," Salem purred softly. "But don't underestimate Circe. She's been scheming for centuries, and not many people have beaten her. She won't just tuck in her tail and turn away."

Sabrina nodded, but she refused to let the cat's warning bring her down. Hilda and Zelda, *and* the Witches' Council, were helping her. What could possibly go wrong?

The cold New England winter followed Sabrina into the halls of Westbridge High, making her feel more vulnerable. Few of the snow flurries touched her, thanks to the spell she had put over her coat, boots, and mittens to seal out the frigid air. The wind gusted through the foyer, stirring up handfuls of snow that lingered on the mats. She took off her scarf in the hallway and dropped it into her coat pocket.

"Sabrina! Hey, wait up!"

Turning, Sabrina watched Valerie twist through the front door.

Dark-haired and pretty, Valerie hurried over to Sabrina, her cheeks flaming from the cold. She shivered dramatically. She brushed at the snowflakes clinging to her eyebrows. "How come none of the snow is hanging on your coat?"

Sabrina's spell actually kept the snow from touching her clothing. "I brushed it off in the foyer."

"You must have done a good job." Valerie made a point of examining Sabrina's coat. "I don't see any snow at all."

Sabrina started walking toward their lockers, not wanting Valerie to focus on her too much. "So how did your date go last night?"

Valerie rolled her eyes. "I'm swearing off arranged blind dates."

"That bad, huh?" Sabrina asked. "I thought Micah Dawes was supposed to be a hunk." The boy went to another high school, and the date had been arranged through mutual friends as well as a school receptionist at Westbridge High.

"Oh, he was a hunk all right," Valerie said in disgust. "Remember what I told you? Captain of the football team and one of the best speakers on the debate team?"

"Yes. Sounded like a really great date: a good-looking guy who can hold up his end of a conversation." Arriving at her locker, Sabrina opened it and took out her first-hour books.

"Sure, the problem is he can hold up his end of the conversation, your end, and pretty much the ends of everyone else who happens to be around."

"Bummer," Sabrina said.

Valerie brushed a stray lock of hair off her face. "It gets worse. Guess what Micah Dawes's favorite subject is?"

Sabrina frowned sympathetically. "Micah Dawes."

"Bingo. When it comes to interesting dates, my luck's holding steady. All bad."

Sabrina felt sorry for Valerie. Although cute, spunky, and vivacious, her friend somehow just didn't quite make a romantic connection that lasted. Most simply fizzled, if there were any sparks at all. "How was the movie?"

The halls started to fill up, and the level of the noise around them required them to speak louder. Despite the way things were so normal, Sabrina couldn't quite shake the dread that clung to her. She still heard Circe's voice in her head. *"I'll take that which you care about most. Then we'll see how untouched you are."*

"The movie was an Agent Richard Brisk adventure," Valerie replied. "Sean Templeton was a hunk, as always, and had about as many secret agent gizmos as Wile E. Coyote in a Road Runner cartoon."

"That sounds like fun." Harvey had mentioned seeing the movie Valentine's Day weekend. Sabrina had liked all the Richard Brisk adventures.

"Micah liked the car," Valerie said. "He liked the motorcycle, and he liked the hovercraft. On the way back to my house you'd have thought he was practicing for the *Grand Prix*. I had my seat belt on tight enough to stop my circulation, but he didn't get a clue. Or maybe he didn't care."

"You went straight home?" Sabrina asked in disbelief. "No pit stop at the Slicery for a soft drink?"

"Nope. I'd heard all the Micah Dawes stories he wanted to tell. And he had to get back to the gym to pump some iron with the rest of the guys. I told him I was into physical fitness too. I know I sounded pretty pathetic." Valerie colored in embarrassment and dropped her eyes.

"What did he say?"

"He said he was glad I was starting on a program. That weight lifting cured a lot of anorexia cases."

"Not cool." Although she really felt bad for Valerie, Sabrina couldn't keep her mind from her own problems. Having to wonder if she was being selfish made her feel even worse. *But*

Micah Dawes can only act like a toad. He can't turn her into one.

"Definitely most uncool," Valerie agreed. "However, I happened to pick up some gossip. Want to hear?"

"Sure." Maybe gossip would prove distracting.

"Guess who's throwing a party the same night the Slicery's putting on the Valentine's Day bash?"

"Libby?"

"Yes. She's decided that something different needs to be offered to make Valentine's Day really special."

Libby Chessler was the head cheerleader at Westbridge High and was one of Sabrina's least favorite people. Libby also decided that she didn't like Sabrina from the first day they had met.

"What kind of party is it going to be?" Sabrina was almost afraid to ask.

"A Hawaiian luau."

"In the middle of New England winter?" Sabrina couldn't believe it. "How does she plan on pulling that off?"

"Her father booked their health club. They have an Olympic-size heated pool and a large spa. The party's going to be catered and feature Hawaiian cuisine, but the guest list is supposed to be very *selective.*"

Sabrina could already guess one of the names

that *wouldn't* be on Libby's list. "How did you find out about the luau?"

"Libby was at the movie," Valerie replied. "I saw Harvey there too."

"My Harvey?" Sabrina asked in surprise.

Valerie raised her eyebrows in surprise. "He's not exactly *your* Harvey these days, is he?"

Sabrina and Harvey had agreed not to be so serious about their dating lately. All the outside pressures of parents, schoolwork, and personal schedules had conspired to tear them apart. But their relationship was too solid not to remain good friends. Maybe more than good friends. There were some things, even with witch powers, that had to be left up to time.

"Nothing's changed," Sabrina answered. "I'm just surprised that Harvey went to the theater alone. We've seen the last two Richard Brisk movies together. I'd assumed we'd be watching this one together too."

"Maybe he found someone else to go with," Valerie suggested.

That possibility hurt more than Sabrina wanted to admit. "Did you see him with anyone else?"

"No. If I had, I would have told you."

"Then he went alone." *There, that feels a little better,* Sabrina thought.

"I can't say that he was alone," Valerie responded. "I only caught a glimpse of him at the food counter. I was with Micah Dawes, remember? He *knows* when he doesn't have your full attention."

Sabrina scanned the halls, feeling agitated. "Have you seen Harvey this morning?"

"Sabrina, I just got here."

"Duh," Sabrina said. "I knew that." She desperately wanted to talk to Harvey. It wasn't fair that she had something else to worry about at the same time Circe was out to get her.

"Hello, weirdlets," a mocking voice said from behind them.

Sabrina turned, knowing things had only gotten worse.

Libby Chessler stood in the hallway with an armful of books. She wore a white coat over white slacks and a long-sleeved white bodysuit. Her dark hair was pulled back from her face, revealing the pink glow of her skin.

Cee Cee and Jill, Libby's closest friends, stood on either side of Libby.

"Hi, Libby." Valerie smiled and took no notice of the insult, as usual. She desperately wanted to become part of the in-crowd at school, and Libby was at the top of that group.

"I guess you've heard about the luau by now," Libby said to Sabrina. "Kind of a neat idea for Valentine's Day, don't you think?"

"I don't know, Libby," Sabrina said. "It's easier to gain weight during the winter. People just aren't as active and tend to eat heavier meals. Maybe waiting till spring would be a better idea. You could scare away a lot of girls who're afraid of swimsuits right now."

Libby laughed. "Cheerleaders *never* have a weight problem, Sabrina. No matter what season it is."

Right, Sabrina thought, *and what would you do if you sprouted a spare tire? Say, sometime between now and Saturday night?* She knew it could be arranged with one tiny little zap. But she curbed the impulse. Libby was only an inconvenience compared to the problems she had now.

"Just think about it," Libby went on. "Valentine's Day, with just an advance preview of the *Sports Illustrated* swimwear issue thrown in for good measure. No guy is going to be able to resist. The party at the Slicery's going to be totally dead."

"Yeah," Cee Cee added, smiling. "A lot of girls are going to be eating their little hearts out all by themselves."

"But I guess you two freakazoids will have to hear about it Monday morning, won't you?" Jill asked. "Because you sure won't be there."

Sabrina restrained her anger. It was easier than usual because Libby really was a minor problem on her list. "I notice you're kind of flushed this morning," she told Libby. "Are you sure you feel okay? You wouldn't want to get sick before the party."

"I'm a little pink from the tanning booth," Libby admitted. "But it's going to be worth it."

"Those UV lamps can really be harsh," Valerie said in an effort to curry favor.

"I know what I'm doing," Libby snapped. "By Saturday, I'll be bronze and to-die-for in my new bikini."

"Valerie's right," Sabrina said. "If you get too much UV exposure, you could be peeling instead of appealing."

Libby only smiled confidently as she walked away.

The bell rang and Sabrina trudged to class, wondering why Harvey had been at the theater and who he'd taken with him.

Harvey Kinkle, who was hardly ever late to class, rushed in after the last bell. Red faced, he slid into a chair nearest the door, two rows from Sabrina, so she couldn't talk to him.

Mrs. Bergman, the English lit teacher, looked at Harvey sternly. She was a skinny bird of a woman with big-lensed glasses and puffy gray hair. "You're late, Mr. Kinkle."

"Yes, ma'am," Harvey apologized. Snow dropped from his coat as he hung it over the back of the chair.

"Usually when we're late," Mrs. Bergman said in her stuffy voice, "we go to the office for an admit slip."

"Yes, ma'am." Harvey stood, gathering his books and coat. "I'll be right back. I'm sorry. I didn't know that was the last bell."

That means you weren't here to hear the first bell, Harvey, Sabrina thought. *Where were you?* Harvey was always there, usually to talk to his friends on the ball teams and to say hello to her. What had made him late?

Or who?

"Sit down, Mr. Kinkle," Mrs. Bergman said, adjusting her glasses. "You are fortunate that the inclement weather makes your tardiness somewhat acceptable this morning. We are feeling magnanimous."

"Yes, ma'am." Harvey returned to his seat with a look of relief. He glanced at Sabrina, then looked away hurriedly as Mrs. Bergman began giving the lesson.

Sabrina couldn't help wondering if Harvey's look had been a guilty one.

☆

Chapter 5

☆

"You were late," Sabrina said to Harvey out in the hall after English lit class ended. The crush of students pushed around them as he walked her to her next class.

Harvey nodded. "Yeah. A little." He didn't offer to explain why, and he seemed preoccupied. "I really thought I was going to be on time."

"Is something wrong?" Sabrina asked.

"No, Sab," he said, using his pet name for her. "I just got a little behind in what I was doing."

Sabrina resisted asking him what he had been doing. In their relationship they'd always been truthful with each other. Thinking of the witch Dashiell and how she'd gotten involved with him without Harvey knowing made her feel guilty, though. Of course, she and Harvey hadn't been officially dating at the time, but she still hadn't let him know till he'd figured it out for himself.

Maybe I'm on the verge of finding out for myself what that feels like, Sabrina thought. She wasn't happy about it. "I missed talking to you this morning."

"Me too, Sab." The smile he gave her was a Harvey original that made her feel good inside.

"When I didn't see you in class, I thought something was wrong."

"No." Harvey shook his head. "I'm trying to get ready for midsemester finals, and dad's been giving me some extra work around the house. The winter's really brutal this year."

"Blame it on El Niño," Sabrina said. "Everybody else does." She noticed Harvey's hands for the first time. They were raw and red and looked as if they'd be painful. "What's wrong with your hands?" She touched one, feeling the deep cold of his fingers.

"Just the cold," Harvey replied.

"That's more than cold." Sabrina reached into her purse and zapped up a tube of healing cream. The cream wasn't a name-brand, but with her magic in it, she knew it would heal fast. She handed the tube to Harvey. "Put that on your hands. It'll make you feel better."

"Sure." He put the tube in his jacket pocket. "I kind of wanted to talk to you about the Valentine's Day party at the Slicery."

Sabrina's heart beat a little faster. "You're still going, aren't you?"

"Yes." Harvey hesitated. "I've got a few things to do on Saturday. But I should be free by the party."

"Okay." Sabrina wanted to say anything but *okay.* However, the next bell was about to ring and Harvey clearly wasn't comfortable saying anything more. He blew on his hands again as they arrived at Sabrina's next class. "Use the cream."

"I will," he said. "Meet me for lunch?"

"Sure. My aunts sent some chicken noodle soup in a thermos. We can split it."

He nodded. "If you're sure there's enough."

"There is." At least there would be when she pointed it up at lunch. She walked into the room feeling confused and letdown. In her relationship with Harvey, they'd never had secrets from each other. Well, he'd never had secrets from her.

That I knew about, she realized. *Maybe it isn't too late to go home sick.*

By lunch everyone was talking about Libby's luau. Although the guest list was guaranteed to be small, most of the student body appeared hopeful about attending.

Sabrina carried the big thermos of chicken noodle soup she'd zapped up after the lunch bell and took a table in the back of the cafeteria.

Hopefully there would be a chance for a little privacy. As an afterthought, when no one was looking, she pointed up two bottles of orange juice as well. If Harvey was coming down with some kind of sickness, she wanted him to have every chance to fight it off.

Of course, faking sickness would be a good way to call off their date Saturday night at the Slicery. She hated that the thought had even entered her mind, but she was really feeling defensive.

"Hey, Sabrina." Valerie hurried over from the lunch counter carrying her tray. "You'll never guess what happened."

"What?" Sabrina tried to sound enthusiastic but didn't have the heart for it.

Valerie plopped onto a seat across the table from Sabrina. Then she noticed the thermos and the two bottles of orange juice. "Are you expecting Harvey?"

"Yes."

"I can go eat with someone else if I'm interrupting something."

Even Valerie thinks something's wrong. Sabrina shook her head. "No. Just sharing lunch. Nothing spectacular. So what's up?"

"Do you know Mark Timmons?"

"The new guy on the tennis team, right?"

"Right." Valerie opened her milk carton and took a sip. "Well, I was thinking, he's probably going to be invited to Libby's party—and he doesn't know many people. So I was thinking about asking him to go to the Slicery. If he ends up getting asked to go to Libby's party, then he'll take me there. What do you think?"

"Sounds like a plan," Sabrina said.

"Now I just have to work up the nerve to ask him." Valerie sighed happily. "You know, there's a really good chance that Libby will invite Harvey. She's always had a thing for him."

Sabrina knew that. Libby had been working on getting Harvey to ask her out since Sabrina first arrived at Westbridge. The reminder started her thinking in a whole new direction. *Maybe Libby invited Harvey to the luau while he was at the theater. He might have accepted, thinking she was going to let me come. Only now he's found out my name isn't on Libby's list.* That could cause a nice guy like Harvey a lot of confusion.

Valerie clapped her hand over her mouth. "Oh my gosh. Open mouth, insert foot. I wasn't thinking."

"It's okay," Sabrina said. "I don't think Harvey's really interested in Libby. Or her party."

"You're probably right." Valerie turned her attention to her plate, picking up a piece of the peanut butter sandwich she had chosen. "Here comes Harvey now." She nodded toward the doorway.

Sabrina watched him enter the cafeteria and get in line for the lunch counter. He didn't even look for her.

"He must have forgotten," Valerie said. She

rose out of her seat before Sabrina could stop her. "Harvey! Hey, Harvey! We're over here!"

Feeling mortified, Sabrina watched as dozens of heads turned in her direction. Harvey looked really embarrassed as he ducked out of the serving line and headed for their table.

"Sorry," he said when he reached them. "I totally forgot."

Hurt and anger filled Sabrina. How could Harvey forget? What did he have on his mind? "It's okay if you'd rather have something on the school menu. Soup really isn't all that extravagant."

"No, that isn't it at all. Soup sounds really good." Harvey sat beside Sabrina and flexed his hands. They still looked raw and red. "I've just had a lot on my mind lately."

Sabrina hated the distance that had developed between them. Back when they'd been going steady, when they'd been able to keep their worlds more tightly intertwined, she had known where his mind was most of the time. Now, she found she had no clue at all. "Anything I can help with?"

"No. It's okay." He opened his hands and looked at them. "That cream seems to be helping, though. Thanks."

"You're welcome." Sabrina uncapped the thermos, then realized she didn't have anything for them to eat out of.

"I'll get some cups," Harvey volunteered. He

got up from the table and walked over to the counter where the condiments and extra silverware were kept. He returned with two Styrofoam cups, spoons, crackers, and napkins.

Sabrina poured the soup into the cups. It was thick and hearty, smelling of goodness, just like the soup Zelda zapped up at the Spellman home when someone wasn't feeling well.

"This is really good soup," Harvey complimented.

Sabrina looked into his brown eyes, noticing for the first time how red they looked. Concern washed away the other feelings. "Are you feeling okay?"

Harvey shrugged. "A little more tired than usual, maybe. It's nothing to worry about."

"This is cold and flu season," Sabrina said. "You have to be careful."

"I am, Sab, really."

She felt guilty as she watched him. Harvey definitely seemed to be sick. He was even paler than he had been that morning, and the red in his eyes looked as if it might have been from a low-grade fever.

"Actually, it could be from the company he's keeping."

Sabrina looked up and found Libby standing behind her. *I need to remember to look through the* Discovery of Magic *book and find out if there's a personal radar spell I can put on myself to detect Libby earlier.*

Before Sabrina could say anything, Libby went on. "Maybe he's reacting to the bracelet you're wearing. Wire and dead weeds isn't just a fashion mistake. They could cause all kinds of allergies to flare up."

Sabrina glanced at her wrist and found the braided wire and leaf bracelet in full view.

"Hey," Harvey said, "that's a cool bracelet. What's it for?"

Sabrina fumbled for an answer, not sure what to say. Then she noticed that everyone in the cafeteria was frozen in place, and the whole room had suddenly gone silent.

She rose from the table, staring at Valerie, who had her sandwich halfway to her lips. Libby stood there with her mouth open, a totally un-Libbylike pose. Knowing that the frozen student body around her was the result of magic, Sabrina glanced around the cafeteria, searching for the person who'd cast the spell. She was afraid she knew.

A prism of neon colors exploded a few feet in front of the line to the lunch counter. It hollowed out, then opened a hole to another realm.

Circe strode through the whirling hypnotic tunnel like a model hitting a runway. Her cropped black hair blew around her head, propelled by cyclonic winds that rushed out at Sabrina. The teenage witch was the only one affected by the magical blast of air. The student body remained untouched.

Circe wore a short-waisted black leather jacket over a midnight blue cami. Tight leather pants showed off her figure, zipping down over her high-heeled boots. Diamonds glinted at her ears and dangled down to her shoulders. She smiled wickedly. "Ah, Sabrina, there you are."

"What are you doing here?" Sabrina demanded, having to shout against the fury of the wind.

"Don't act so surprised," Circe said. "I told you I'd be back. In fact, I gave you fair warning."

Sabrina's eyes teared as she faced the brutal wind. The warm liquid tracked across her temples.

"I know your aunts warded your house," Circe said, gazing around the school. "But even the Witches' Council can't protect you everywhere. You should have stayed home."

Sabrina quickly put a spell together.

> "Magic unite with strength to right the wrongs, send this witch back where she belongs."

She gestured, pushing the flat of her hand with the wire-and-leaf bracelet outward.

Amber lightning leaped from Sabrina's palm, arcing toward Circe.

The ancient witch smirked and flipped a small crimson gem out that intercepted the amber lightning. As soon as gem and lightning touched, they canceled each other out in a blaze of pyrotechnics.

"Not bad," Circe said, "for someone so young who has so much yet to learn."

Gathering herself, Sabrina tried to call home through her magic, but it was like she kept getting a busy signal inside her head. A headache started at the base of her skull.

"You can't get in touch with your aunts," Circe said. "Nor can you contact anyone in the Witches' Council. It's just you and me, little girl."

"What do you want?"

"To humble you, as I've already told you." Circe gazed around the school. "Interesting environs you choose for yourself."

"High school isn't something you choose," Sabrina argued. *"Believe* me."

"You're a witch." Circe moved toward Libby, obviously surveying the cheerleader. "You don't have to attend high school in the mortal realm. Since you turned sixteen, you had your choice of going to school here or in the Other Realm. You chose here."

Actually, Zelda and Hilda had only casually mentioned the possibility of going to school in the Other Realm. The choice had been Sabrina's, and she had chosen to stay in the mortal realm. With so much changing about herself, Sabrina felt it helped her to remain in the world she knew best.

"In my day," Circe went on, "I was hand-picked by my mentor. I trained for years at her side, learning all she knew. When I began to teach her things about her own powers, I chose to go my own way. Perhaps if you'd been trained the old way, you'd have shown me the respect I deserved."

"Respect isn't something that's just given," Sabrina said, "it's also earned."

"Such a sharp tongue. You'll live to regret it." Circe nodded at Libby. "Tell me who this creature is."

"Libby Chessler," Sabrina answered. "My best friend." As soon as she said it, she felt bad. If Circe chose to believe her and followed through on her threat because of it, Sabrina was to blame for whatever happened to Libby.

Before Sabrina could say anything else, Circe turned to her with an upraised palm between them. A fat butterfly with magenta and black wings appeared in a haze of red sparkles and flew away.

"You lie," the ancient witch stated with a smile. She drew her fingers over Libby's face, not quite touching the skin. "Too bad. From what I see of this one, possessing her and having her around would have been—*interesting.* Kindred spirits always are."

Sabrina watched the woman turn from Libby and breathed a sigh of relief. The relief lasted only till Circe turned to Harvey.

"This one, I think," the ancient witch said. She strode purposefully toward Harvey, who was still sitting at the table across from Valerie.

"No!" Sabrina started toward Harvey.

Circe threw up an arm.

Instantly Sabrina felt as if she had run into an invisible brick wall. She stopped within an arm's reach of Harvey.

"Oh, yes," Circe said. "I believe this one is exactly the one I want." She gestured at Harvey.

Harvey shook his head, his eyelids fluttering as if he had just awakened. He stood up and looked around. "Hey, Sab." He paused and smiled big. "Don't know why I'm talking to you, though. This is just a dream, right? So that means you're really not here."

"Quiet," Circe snapped.

Harvey shrugged. "Sure."

Sabrina reached for him, thinking she could protect him with the spell on the bracelet if she could only touch him. "Harvey, come over here."

"No, Harvey," Circe ordered. "You'll be coming with me."

Harvey looked at the ancient witch. "Sure." Then he turned his attention to Sabrina and gave her one of his shy smiles. "Sorry, Sab. Gotta go." He joined Circe, standing just behind her.

"Harvey!" Sabrina called.

"You lose," Circe mocked. She gestured and a silver chain suddenly appeared in her hand. The other end of it was attached to a heavy brass collar that had appeared around Harvey's neck. "Remember your losses, little girl, and think twice before you offer disrespect to one who is your better."

Sabrina's heart pounded in her chest as she watched Circe lead Harvey into the mouth of the tunnel. The invisible wall held the teenage witch back; not even the bracelet would let her break through.

Circe held the chain firmly, stopping Harvey in his tracks. He turned and waved to Sabrina, a smile on his lips. "What a cool dream. See you soon, huh?"

Tears filled Sabrina's eyes as she watched the tunnel close, then disappear in a neon haze. Before she drew her next breath, the lunchroom returned to normal.

The only thing missing was Harvey Kinkle.

Sabrina found herself sitting at her table, watching Valerie take the first bite of her sandwich. Instead of two cups of soup, only one sat on the table. All trace of Harvey's presence had been removed.

"Have you seen Harvey?" she asked Valerie.

Valerie shook her head. "He wasn't here during first period. You were there. Unless you've seen him."

"No," Sabrina said. "I haven't seen him." *Maybe I won't ever see him again.*

Chapter 6

"You need to calm down."

"This *is* calm," Sabrina replied. She was in the Spellman kitchen with her aunts. "We can't just sit here and do nothing."

"We're not going to, honey," Hilda said, taking a seat on the opposite side of the table from Sabrina. "Zelda and I have been talking to the Witches' Council all day. We think we know where Circe is now."

"I thought everybody knew that."

"Not exactly," Zelda said. "The Other Realm provides more inconsistent physical laws than the mortal realm does. Our spells here are affected by a thousand different immutable cause-and-effect relationships. We all know that Circe has created a pocket world for herself, but no one knows where it is. She gets her witch-mail forwarded to a service."

"So, you think Harvey's lost?" Sabrina asked.

"He's not lost," Zelda said in her calmest voice. "We know where to start looking for Circe's pocket world. We just don't have a way in. We also have to know how things were left at school."

"When Circe took Harvey, she erased everybody's memory of him," Sabrina said, controlling the fear that ran rampant inside her. "No one thinks he came to school today. I zapped up a note about a dental appointment and turned it in to the school secretary. Then I came home."

Salem leaped from the kitchen counter to the table. "I've got a friend that can maybe help us find Circe."

"Who?" Sabrina asked.

"Bajher," the cat answered.

"I didn't know he was still around." Zelda didn't look happy about the prospect. "And even if he is still around, I don't know that we'd want to get involved with him."

"Who're you kidding?" Salem grumbled. "This is something right up Bajher's alley. And trust me, in the last few years, I've become something of an expert regarding alleys."

"Salem's right, you know," Hilda said. "If anybody can get past Circe's defenses, it'd be Bajher."

"The Witches' Council isn't going to be happy

about our involving ourselves with Bajher," Zelda pointed out.

"Aunt Zelda, this is Harvey we're talking about," Sabrina pleaded. "And it's all my fault she's got him."

"This is Bajher's kind of thing," Salem stated. "You know it and I know it."

Sabrina could always tell when Zelda was giving in—her aunt's face broadcast it. Of course, Zelda often didn't give in.

"All right," Zelda said. "Everybody go up to the linen closet and let's leave before I have time to regret this."

"Who *is* this guy?" Sabrina asked, peering around the huge cave they'd popped into. Massive computers covered the rough-hewn stone walls of the cave, but they weren't like any computers she had ever seen. A stream sluicing down one wall turned a water wheel connected to one computer, while a boiling cauldron heating in the center of the floor powered three others by steam engines. Gerbils and squirrels ran on tracks, powering others. A scarlet-and-gold macaw sat in a wire cage hanging from the ceiling in the center of the room.

Looking at the haphazard arrangement of working computers and listening to the asthmatic wheezes they made, Sabrina felt doubt gnawing at her confidence. She didn't see how someone with computer equipment straight out of the Flintstones could help her rescue Harvey. The belts the squirrels and gerbils ran on squeaked and screeched in protest.

"He's a renegade," Zelda answered. "Much of what he's doing here is against the Witches' Council bylaws."

Salem leaped to a work station near one of the big computer banks and watched the racing gerbil team with bright-eyed interest. "The man's a genius. In the Other Realm, Bajher was a witch's equivalent of a ninety-eight-pound weakling. His attention deficit disorder kept him from any advanced spell work in *The Discovery of Magic*. Then he discovered Charles Babbage and helped work on developing the first computers. They exist easily in the mortal realm, but in the Other Realm their logic base is different and usually won't work the same way."

Sabrina glanced around the cavern. "Where is he?"

"Probably up in his rooms," Hilda said. "He doesn't keep regular hours." She walked over to the macaw in its cage and pulled one of the bird's tailfeathers.

The macaw opened its mouth. Sabrina expected the bird to screech, but a deep, bonging doorbell sound came out of its beak instead.

"Bajher was always a funny guy." Salem laughed in appreciation.

A *ping* sounded as the witch zapped into the room. He was tall and thin, with thick-lensed glasses and dark hair that looked as if it hadn't been combed in days. He had a mustache and goatee and wore a long white lab coat over a drooping yellow muscle shirt, orange running shorts that revealed thin, pale legs, and lime green flip-flops. The plastic pocket protector in the breast pocket of his lab coat had a name tag that read BAJHER.

He blinked owlishly behind the thick lenses, then settled his gaze on Salem and Hilda. He smiled and walked toward Hilda, taking her hands in his. "Hilda, it's so nice to see you again." His German accent was surprising. "You've stayed avay so long, you naughty girl. Vhat haff you been doing mit yourself?"

"Oh, you know." Hilda shrugged and took her hands back, wiping them on her slacks but trying hard not to be obvious about it. "The usual. Just a lot more of it than normal."

"I thought you vere going to come see me again."

"I intended to, but I had to wash my hair."

"Oh." Bajher blinked again, looking perplexed. "Vell, it looks very nice, and I'm glad that you're here now."

"This isn't exactly a social call," Hilda said. "We need your help."

Bajher spread his hands, his smile more certain this time. "But of course. Vhatever you need, I vill only be too glad to assist you."

"Good," Hilda said, "because we need to spy on Circe."

Bajher's pale complexion got even paler. "Vhat?"

The techno-witch wasn't happy about the assignment, but Sabrina had to admit once Bajher applied himself, he got things done quickly. "Vhy didn't the Vitches' Council take care of this?" Bajher asked as he tapped the keyboard in front of him.

"They tried," Hilda answered. "They conjured up a bracelet to protect Sabrina, and we warded the house against her, but there was no way to cast spells on everything."

"Circe's also an Ancient," Zelda put in. "The witches' code of ethics doesn't really apply to her."

"She's going to haff her pocket vorld deeply covered by security, you know," Bajher said irritably.

"That's why we came to you," Hilda said. "If anyone could have found her, Zelda would have found her on the labtop we have at home."

Zelda rolled her eyes at her sister.

Hilda made a what-was-I-supposed-to-say grimace back at her.

Sabrina ignored the exchange. Both her aunts were working hard to help her save Harvey despite the personality differences they had. She peered over Bajher's shoulder at the computer screen.

A sickly green wave spread out into a prismatic hourglass form that toppled end over end against a background of purple clouds. Upon closer inspection, Sabrina spotted the dozen lizard-lidded eyeballs rolling through the hourglass shape. "Lizard's eyes?"

"Eyes of newt," Zelda corrected. "It's a base ingredient in a number of long-distance scrying spells."

"They are held in a representation of a Möbius strip," Bajher said. "Eyes of newt suspended in a never-ending planar shape. A combination of old vitchcraft and technology. Nothing can mitstand the power I'm using here."

"Are you sure it's working?" Sabrina asked.

"Yes, it's vorking," Bajher snapped. "I've got it up to full power now." And it *was* true that he'd added an extra squirrel-driven belt team to the computer's power source. "I'm searching all the known realms now, and adding in the possibilities derived from those. Even the Other Realm is finite, you know. There can only be so many areas vhere Circe could haff hidden her personal vorld avay."

The hourglass continued tumbling on the computer screen, growing increasingly smaller, but the newts' eyes pressed against the glass, some of them blinking excitedly. Without warning, though, a vine suddenly streaked out across the screen and seized the hourglass.

"Ah," Bajher said.

"Ah?" Sabrina repeated. "What does 'ah' mean?"

"It means I tripped across somevon's security system," Bajher replied.

"Circe's?"

"That's who ve're looking for, isn't it?" The techno-witch hunched over his keyboard, more determined. In brief seconds the vine shredded into thousands of pieces. "Ve're past the outer perimeter of the vorld. Ve should be getting a glimpse of it at any moment."

The hourglass exploded on the screen without warning, breaking up into thousands of pieces and scattering newts' eyes in all directions. The eyes caught fire and crisped.

"Yum," Salem said. "Barbecue."

"Now that," Bajher stated, "is something I've not encountered before." He tapped more keys in rapid succession. A second hourglass began the plunge through the purple cloud, picking up where the first one had left off.

The purple cloud gave way to a forest. The hourglass swung under the trees, narrowly avoiding moving branches in the shape of claws. Sabrina stared at the angry faces on some of the trees as the hourglass shot by.

"Is that forest real?" she asked.

Bajher shook his head, making his tousled hair

jump. "No. That is merely a representation of the magic she's employed to keep her vorld safe from prying eyes."

Abruptly, a branchy hand swiped at the scrying device, obliterating it. Newts' eyes bounced from the trees but were quickly grabbed by the hands.

"She is good," the techno-wizard stated. He sounded appreciative as he tapped the keyboard again and created another scrying device. "This is our last attempt for a vhile."

"What are you talking about?" Sabrina asked.

"These are my best hacking spellgrams," Bajher answered. "If I can't hack my vay through mit these, ve are shtumped."

"Shtumped!" Sabrina couldn't believe it. "Ve—*We* can't be shtumped! Harvey's over there!"

Hilda put a comforting hand on the teenage witch's shoulder. "Everything's going to be okay. Bajher is the best there is." She directed her attention to the techno-wizard. "Aren't you, Bajher?"

He ran a hand through his tousled hair and adjusted his thick glasses. A coy smile flashed on his lips as he glanced at Hilda. "All this for bowling, dinner, and a movie? I need to be inspired."

"Bowling," Hilda offered.

Bajher shook his head. "I don't feel inspired."

"This is no time to be haggling," Hilda snapped.

Pointing at the screen, Bajher said, "Look. I am almost there. Only a little farther. But the vay vill not be easy."

"Hilda," Zelda prompted.

Hilda made a face and stamped her foot. "Oh, all right. But if you don't get in there you're going to spend the next week as a toad. With fever blisters." She smiled prettily. "Feel inspired now?"

"Oh, yes, my little *liebchen."* Bajher turned to his task, darting a quick glance at the squirrels on the drive belt. He pointed at them.

Immediately the squirrels and belts doubled in size. The ratcheting screams of the tortured ball bearings on the track filled the cave. Smoke and sparks shot from the back of the computer.

"Banzai!" Bajher yelled as he attacked the keyboard.

Sabrina watched the computer screen, worried that it was going to explode at any second.

☆

Chapter 7

☆

The computer shook and shivered and continued spitting out smoke and sparks. Through it all, Bajher laughed maniacally, squirming back and forth across his seat as he continued attacking the keyboard. His eyes widened behind the thick lenses of his glasses.

"I am the best!" he crowed. "Neither magic nor technology can hold me back! I am a ghost, an eel, and the tongue of a llama, able to go anyvhere I please!"

In the next instant, the computer screen cleared the forest. The view changed to a very familiar metropolitan skyline filled with tall buildings at the edge of a large river.

"Ve are here," Bajher announced.

"Manhattan Island?" Zelda asked. "Circe lives in New York City?"

"I'm trading bowling, dinner, and a movie for that?" Hilda asked.

"Nonononononono," Bajher disagreed. "Do not be fooled. That is not the New York City you know." He tapped the keyboard again and the view on the screen changed. "See? There is the Empire State Building, but vhere are the Vorld Trade Center towers?"

Sabrina studied the cityscape, but found she didn't know enough about the area to know what was missing. She'd been to New York on shopping sprees with her aunts, but not nearly enough to know her way around.

"He's right," Zelda said. "There are differences."

"Of course there are," Bajher said proudly. "This is an alternate Manhattan, a shadow of the true Manhattan ve know. Vatch and I shall show you."

The computer screen magnified the view, scanning the streets. Sabrina was astounded by the difference. Instead of streets cluttered with pedestrians and cars, they were cluttered with animals and things that didn't look quite human. Horse-drawn carriages and hansom cabs flowed in both directions, but it wasn't the bumper-to-bumper traffic she remembered from her visits to Manhattan.

A teenage boy with the elongated beak of a duck and wings stood on one streetcorner hawking newspapers. A man bought a paper from the duck-boy but had trouble getting money out of his wallet because he had cloven hands.

A centaur in a cop's blue uniform patrolled the sidewalk, swinging his billy club. A red-furred orangutan dealt three cards out across a portable table, moving the cards around with all four hands while an alligator-man, a woman with zebra striping and a short-cropped mane, and a man with turkey tailfeathers sticking out of his pants and scratching his red, wattled neck watched.

More animal people and supernatural creatures filled the stores and streets open to view.

"Who are all those people?" Sabrina asked.

"Other victims," Zelda answered. "Circe is very unforgiving and imagines all kinds of insults. But I had no idea that there were so many people she'd put spells on. The Witches' Council needs to be made aware of this."

Sabrina remembered from her research about the ancient witch that Circe had kept all her victims on an island. "In *The Odyssey,* Homer wrote that Circe lived on an island," she said. "And Manhattan is an island too. Rivers are on either side of it." She couldn't remember the names, but she thought she'd once learned them for a geography test. Who knew? Names were constantly being changed on maps anyway, and even the lines didn't stay in the same places. *And Harvey's down there in that mess somewhere.* "So what's the importance of islands to Circe?"

"In the old days, back when witchcraft was first beginning," Zelda said, "there were places of power. Places where witches lived or worked that allowed them access to power."

"Right," Hilda added. "Merlin was one of the first to recognize the significance of spatial spell structure and stacking."

Bajher shrugged. "Even here, I chose my location because of overlapping magnetic fields from the mortal vorld and from spell fallout in the Other Realm. Placement can be very important."

"Later witches weren't tied to the land, though," Zelda said. "We sort of learned to tune into the spell frequencies wherever they are. Circe should be able to do that too."

"But you haff to admit," Bajher said, "in this pocket vorld she has created for herself, she is very powerful. No one outside of myself could possibly have penetrated her defenses."

"Enough with the speculation," Sabrina said. "Harvey's over there, and for all I know he's dreaming about chasing rabbits or growing fur, feathers, or scales. We need to go get him."

"Ve?" Bajher asked, taking his thick glasses off and cleaning them. "There is no *ve* in this operation. Circe's defenses are very precise. You've seen for yourselves how complicated it is even to scry on her. Getting somevun in, vhy that vould be next to impossible."

"We can't go after Harvey?" Sabrina stared at

the maze of buildings that made up the alternate Manhattan.

"I didn't say that. I only said that *ve* couldn't do it. According to my calculations, I can transport any object veighing less than vun hundred twenty-five pounds into that realm mitout getting caught."

"Well," Hilda said unhappily, "that lets one of us out."

Zelda sighed and shook her head, folding her arms across her chest. "Two of us."

"Two?" Hilda said. "I thought that new diet was—"

"It is," Zelda replied. "But slowly."

"You told me you'd lost twelve pounds," Hilda said.

"I did."

Hilda's eyes popped open. "Then you lied to me about what you weighed?"

"Hilda, grow up," Zelda snapped. "Since when have we ever been honest with each other about our weight?"

"I'll go," Sabrina said.

Both her aunts looked at her.

"Into Circe's realm by yourself?" Zelda said.

"I don't think so," Hilda added. "Your father would kill us. I can just hear Ted's response."

"Look," Sabrina said, "Harvey's over there and it's my fault. I'm going."

Zelda turned to Bajher. "What if Hilda and I

shrank ourselves down to pocket size? Couldn't we be sent over with Sabrina then?"

Bajher shook his head. "There are no conversion controls on this spellgram. You go as you are, or you don't go at all."

"I'm going," Sabrina said again.

The techno-wizard looked at her over his glasses. "You veigh less than vun hundred twenty-five pounds?"

"It's the coat." Sabrina took the garment off and regretted it immediately. "See?"

"Step on the scale." Bajher pointed at the floor and a large swordfish popped into view, wriggling enthusiastically and arcing high into the air.

"Dinner!" Salem exclaimed, poising to leap at the flopping fish.

"Hilda," Bajher said, scooting his chair away from the big fish.

Hilda pointed and zapped the fish away. It was too late to stop Salem's leap and he landed on the digital scale that materialized in the swordfish's place.

"No," the cat whined. "Bring it back. It's not fair." The digital readout flickered and came to a rest on nine pounds.

"Move off the scale, please," the techno-witch instructed.

Still miffed, Salem stepped off the scale.

"I only weigh a hundred and eight pounds,"

Sabrina protested. "I know it, so there's no reason to step on the scale."

"Young lady," Bajher stated, "a spellgram is a very precise thing. The slightest deviation—*poof!*—off you go and I haff no idea vhere."

"Poof!" Sabrina repeated. *I don't like the sound of that at all.*

"And no idea vhere," Bajher said. "Maybe ve get you back, maybe ve don't. These pocket vorlds are very tricky things, you know."

Sabrina didn't, but she took his word for it. Reluctantly, she stepped onto the scale. The digital readout spun, the ruby numbers flickering. Her aunts and Bajher, even Salem, leaned in to look.

"One hundred fourteen pounds," Salem said, raising his head to look at her. Then he shook it from side to side. Bajher peered at her over his glasses.

"The scales are off," Sabrina argued. "That's the only answer. And these shoes are really heavy. I'll take them off."

"No no no." Bajher held up a hand. "You veigh less than vun hundred twenty-five pounds. Everything is okay."

"But I *don't* weigh one hundred fourteen pounds," Sabrina told him.

"Lying about your weight must be a hereditary defect," Salem observed.

"Careful, furball," Hilda warned. "You're not

exactly lean and mean yourself, and I don't think you've been properly wormed in a while."

Salem held up his paws. "Not another word on the subject of worming." He shuddered. "The Spanish Inquisition invented worming, didn't it?"

"It is okay, Sabrina." Bajher tapped on the keyboard. "No problem. I'll get you into Circe's vorld."

"Do you know where she is?" Zelda asked.

"Yes. She's there." He tapped the screen, indicating the tallest building in the cityscape. "On the eighty-sixth floor of the Umpire State Building."

"The *Umpire* State Building?" Hilda asked.

Bajher tapped the controls and brought the front of the building into view. There, marked clearly in tall letters, was the name UMPIRE STATE BUILDING. On top, next to a moored dirigible floating in the breeze, was the statue of a baseball umpire with his fist theatrically clenched and raised. The dirigible was shaped like a bear's face and had letters on the side: Goodbear Blimp. The gondola floated freely below.

Sabrina focused on the information she was most interested in. "Circe lives in the Umpire State Building on the eighty-sixth floor, right?"

"Technically," Bajher replied, consulting a pull-down menu. "She owns the whole building, but her residential quarters are located on the eighty-sixth floor."

"Then that's where I'll look for her," Sabrina said. "How soon can I get over there?"

"As soon as you're ready."

"But you're not ready yet," Zelda said. "We're going to equip you." She narrowed her eyes and set to work with zeal.

Ten minutes later Sabrina was loaded down with survival gear: camouflage clothes, a football helmet, rope, rations, and a bulky first-aid kit that could have housed a family of raccoons.

"Stop! Stop!" Bajher protested. "This is never going to vork!"

"I'll say." Sabrina dropped the gear to the computer cave's floor. "If I need anything, I'll just zap it up when I get over there."

"Not a good idea," Bajher declared. "Anytime you use your magic, Circe vill know."

"Okay," Sabrina replied. "Then just put me as close to Harvey as you can and I'll go get him, then zap us back."

"What about the weight limit for Harvey?" Hilda asked.

"Coming back," Bajher said, "it's no problem if Circe knows ve've penetrated her security. It is designed to keep things out, and in doing that, it has a veakness ve can exploit to get things back out again."

"Then why not just zap Harvey back?"

"Because he is under her spell. I need to send somevun over who can create a spell of her own."

Sabrina started to point at the camouflage uniform, then asked Bajher, "What's the weather like over there?"

The techno-witch opened a small menu on the computer screen and made a selection. "High seventies, vith a chance of rain this evening. Mild vind."

"Terrific." Sabrina pointed herself up a pair of cargo shorts, a baby blue tank with a blue-and-khaki sheer shirt jacket to pull it together, then added sunglasses with metallic blue lenses and turbo flip-flops. As an afterthought, she pointed up a plaid blue-and-caramel hemp and cord backpack.

"Very touristy," Salem said. "But you're not exactly going to fit in with the local population."

"I could zap myself a chicken head or something," Sabrina offered. *Ugh! That's a terrible idea.* But she knew her aunts were wavering on their decision to let her go.

"No," Zelda said. "A chicken's vision is too restrictive and takes too long to get used to."

Hilda looked at her in surprise.

"Oh come on," Zelda sighed. "Surely you remember Uncle Marty, Great-Aunt Claire's third husband. Your fourth birthday party?"

Hilda smiled. "Oh, yes. I can't believe I'd forgotten that. He was a riot."

"Not if you were the chicken," Zelda assured her. She held her hand up and a compact appeared in her fingers. "Take this."

Sabrina took the compact and opened it, checking her makeup. "Have I got something on my face?"

"No. The compact's a flip-phone that will connect you to us here. Look into the mirror."

Sabrina looked. After only a moment her image cleared and left her staring at the cave.

"It's scrambled and set for burst transmission," Zelda said.

"The guy you dated in the National Security Agency?" Hilda asked.

"I didn't know he was an information specialist until later," Zelda admitted. "I thought he was just a computer specialist. But he had some interesting toys."

"Cool," Sabrina said, listening to her aunts in stereo as their voices came over the compact.

"Not exactly state-of-the-art *Mission: Impossible,"* Salem groused. "I can't imagine Tom Cruise using a compact to phone home. E.T. either."

Sabrina couldn't either, and didn't want to try.

"Circe may not be able to intercept your communications transmission," Bajher said, "but she may be able to track it. If you use it, don't stay on long, and keep moving."

"Okay," Sabrina said. "Then I guess I'm ready

to go. Zap me into the Umpire State Building, I'll grab Harvey, and we'll be right back."

"It von't be that easy," the techno-witch said. "The closer I put you to the Umpire State Building, the more intense Circe's varning systems are going to be."

"Really close is not a good idea, then. So how close can you get me and I'll still be safe?"

Bajher consulted another menu and pulled up a Manhattan map on the computer screen. "Chinatown?"

"Chinatown's three miles from the Empire—uh, Umpire State Building," Hilda objected. "Surely you can do better than that."

"Yes," the techno-witch agreed. "And getting her closer vill, of course, increase the risk. Exponentially."

"Chinatown," Sabrina grumped. "I'll hoof it."

"Get caught by Circe," Salem warned, "and that could be the case exactly." Despite the tension of the moment, he burst out laughing. "I crack myself up sometimes."

No one else laughed.

"And if you do get caught and Circe turns you into a fish," the cat went on, "be sure you demand payment to scale." He howled with mirth.

"Salem," Hilda said in a warning tone.

"Okay," he said in disdain, "I'll quit. I know when I've gone too—too *fur!*" Before he could complete his latest round of laughter, Zelda zapped a muzzle on him. He flopped his head and tried to get out of it.

"You know," Zelda said, "it occurs to me that at a hundred and fourteen pounds, Sabrina is well within the weight limits of the spellgram."

"Those scales were off," Sabrina said.

Hilda picked up her sister's thought. "Nine pounds could easily go along for the ride."

Salem's eyes above the muzzle popped into wide alertness. He shook his head from side to side.

"Oh, yes," Zelda said.

"Uh," Sabrina interjected, "I really think this is a bad idea."

"Salem knows Manhattan," Hilda pointed out. "Before he tried to take over the world thirty years ago, he tried taking over high finance and spent a lot of time on Wall Street."

"It was never actually proven," Zelda said, "but there were a number of witches who lost fortunes in 1929, when the market crashed, who believe to this day that Salem had a hand in it."

Salem shook his head again, paws digging at the muzzle. Finally he gave up and sat whining and crying plaintively through the muzzle.

"Stop begging," Hilda said. "It's not going to work this time. We can't go with Sabrina and someone should. What kind of familiar are you?" She zapped the muzzle away.

"A scared one," he admitted.

"It's all right," Sabrina said, feeling sorry for her pet. "He doesn't have to go." *And having Salem around always seems to complicate matters. Harvey's situation is complicated enough.*

"Salem," Zelda said in a soft voice, "I'll give you a choice: go with Sabrina or it'll be Dr. Zachary's Fat Felines Fun Farm for the summer. And you know what the diets are like there."

"You'd subject my delicate palate to that?"

"Are there any doubts?" Zelda asked.

"Okay," the cat grumbled. "I'm going." With a single fluid motion, he leaped into Sabrina's waiting arms. "But you owe me big time for this."

"We'll knock off some of the goodwill debt you owe us," Hilda said graciously.

"Now we're ready," Sabrina told Bajher.

The techno-witch tapped on the computer keyboard again. Immediately a rectangular screen appeared in front of Sabrina. It glowed a brilliant and beautiful blue green and shimmered as she watched it. The static electricity pulled at her hair. She pointed up a floppy plaid hat that matched her backpack. As an extra bonus, the crushability of the hat guaranteed no hat-head. She zapped her hair into a braid and tucked it under the hat.

"Valk through," Bajher said, "and I'll get you into Circe's vorld."

Sabrina took a deep breath. The fear touched her then, her stomach cramping up. She glanced at her aunts. "Well, gotta go." She stepped into the rippling blue-green energy field and discovered it was as cold as a plunge into an Arctic pool. "Next stop, Chinatown."

"It's not exactly Chinatown," Bajher warned. "According to the map I'm looking at, it's called Chiatown."

Chiatown? Sabrina thought. Then the darkness swept over her and took her away.

☆

Chapter 8

☆

Once he was a normal housecat. A fun-loving, tuna-munching pet. A pet who'd given up dreams of world conquest for the teen witch he had befriended. But now, he was forced upon a journey he never wished to make, going to strange lands, on a predestined collision directly into—*'The Twilight Zone!'* "

Sabrina tried to ignore Salem's Rod Serling voice-over as she stepped through the blue-green rectangle at the other end of the trip. Cool summer wind washed over her and street sounds filled the area around her.

"I offer for your rumination," Salem continued, "one Salem Saberhagen. Cat. Friend. *Sacrificial lamb."*

"Enough," Sabrina ordered. She'd never been to Chinatown in the mortal-realm Manhattan, but the decor in this neighborhood was definitely Oriental. Open-air restaurants sat on either side of the narrow street. Vegetables and cages of live chickens occupied a marketplace farther down the thoroughfare.

While the appearance of the area was Oriental, the neighborhood's inhabitants were even more exotic. Sabrina understood immediately why it had been renamed Chiatown.

Every person she saw, and there were a number of them, looked like a walking, talking Chiapet. They came in different sizes and shapes, but all of them possessed the telltale clumps of green vegetation growing from their heads, hands, and bodies. A few of them were already flowering tiny white-and-yellow blooms that looked kind of festive.

Except that everyone was busy scratching at the clumps.

"Do I smell catnip?" Salem asked. He pushed his head through Sabrina's arms. "Oh, now those are some majorly *ugly* hairdos. Do they brush those, or do they roto-till them?"

Sabrina's sudden entrance through the shimmering blue-green portal attracted notice, but not attention. *Of course with Circe living here, maybe they're all used to people popping in and out of the neighborhood.*

But she really couldn't see the ancient witch casually strolling through the people she'd captured over the years. Even with her guy-rilla guards.

The fruit stand vendor, a huge donkey that stood on his back legs and adjusted apples with his blunt foot, followed Sabrina's approach. Flowers sprouted from saddlebags across his back and from a mane that hung over his eyes and ran down his neck to the saddlebags. His tail consisted of a plumed spray of long green grasses.

"Can I help you?" he asked, waving his blunt foot at the apples, oranges, pears, and bananas on his cart.

The clop-clop-clopping of hooves against the street surface created an undercurrent of sound that was almost music. Then Sabrina noticed the absence of car horns as well as other car noises. *This Manhattan is much quieter than the real one.*

"I hope so," Sabrina said. "I was wondering what was the quickest way to the Umpire State Building."

Two small Chiapet puppies erupted from the magazine shop behind the fruit vendor and chased each other, biting at the moss on the other's head. Salem hissed at them reflexively, which only made the Chiapet puppies laugh.

"There's the subway," the fruit peddler said. "Or, if you've got the money, there's always a Yellow Cab. Except on days that it's raining. You can never seem to get a cab on rainy days. I'm surprised that you ask, though."

"Why?"

"You could always just zap yourself there. Circe zaps herself all around the city."

"I kind of want to surprise her," Sabrina admitted.

"Is it her birthday?"

"Not that I know of. Why?"

The Chiapet donkey shrugged. "It's probably the only day she hasn't declared as a holiday. We just figured she was keeping it from us so we wouldn't pay attention to the fact that she's getting older." He adjusted a couple of coconuts. "Of course, since she's a witch, she's not really getting any older, is she?"

"No."

"But then, neither are the rest of us," the Chiapet donkey said. "I met a cow a few weeks ago at an EARS support group meeting that has been here over two thousand years."

"EARS?" Sabrina echoed.

"Yeah. It's an acronym for Enspelled And Readjusting Society." He reached up and brushed at his own long ears, covered with a light dusting of plant material. "Funny how little attention you paid to them back in the real world, but everybody has them here." He pointed to Salem. "Are you here about your friend?"

"My friend?"

"I noticed Circe did a full conversion on him. She doesn't do that very often these days. Can he still think?"

"I can also talk, Astro-turf," Salem growled.

The Chiapet donkey shook his head. "Don't think you're going to hang on to that ability. There are a lot of other people here who are now animals, but they can't think anymore. They're just—well—*animals.*"

Sabrina knew from her experience with Macdougal, the golden retriever Harvey had cared for a short time back, that animals could be quite thoughtful. Especially after she'd accidentally exchanged Harvey's body with Macdougal's. But she didn't want to argue the point. "I'm not here about Salem."

"You like him as a cat?"

"I think he's fine as a cat," Sabrina answered. "I couldn't think of a better cat to have." *Most of the time,* she added to herself.

Salem preened in her arms, arching his back and rubbing against her.

The Chiapet donkey grimaced, which was kind of hard to pull off with green mossy growth hanging between his widely spaced eyes. "It's people like you who really don't help matters for the Enspelled And Readjusting Society. Too apathetic, too accepting."

"I've got a friend here," Sabrina said. "Salem

being a cat has nothing to do with Circe. But I want to save my friend."

"When did your friend come over?"

"A couple hours ago."

The Chiapet donkey shrugged. "Then he or she's probably already a goatboy by now. You ought to go home while you still can. You'll always be able to get another friend."

"Now who's being apathetic?" Sabrina asked sharply. *No way can I replace Harvey.* The sheer thought of it almost broke her heart.

"You can't fight City Hall, I always say. And here, Circe is City Hall. You don't leave well enough alone, she'll send the guy-rillas after you."

"How long have you been here?" Sabrina asked.

"Since the eighties. That's when Circe went through her turn-humans-who-cramp-my-style-into-Chiapets phase."

Sabrina looked around, amazed at the number of people who were Chiapets. "This is all from the eighties?" *How many people had Circe ensorcelled over the years?* she wondered. Then she realized she had an answer: enough to populate a large metropolitan area.

"Yes. And you might ask yourself, why Chiapets? The answer is simple. Circe just isn't all that inventive."

"Why hasn't anyone ever protested?"

"Oh, we have. But you get attached to the

ability to stand on your two back feet and talk. That's only the first thing Circe takes away."

"Couldn't you leave?"

The Chiapet donkey shook his head. "Even if we could get past the lake monsters in the river, where would we go? A sideshow in a circus? *The Tonight Show* with Johnny Carson? *Geraldo?* A life as a permanent talk-show freak guest isn't something I'd want."

"Carson's left the show now," Sabrina said.

"You're kidding. Man, I loved his monologues."

"Jay Leno took over for him."

"The kid with the big face? You're kidding."

"No."

"Maybe things have changed on the talk-show circuit. I could talk to a few of the guys, see about getting back to the mortal realm. Maybe there's a way to franchise this thing."

"I don't know about that," Sabrina said.

"I'll give it some more thought." The Chiapet donkey shifted the fruit again. "You know what I miss most?"

"No."

He held his legs out. "Hands. You never know how much you're going to miss them till they're gone. I get itches, and I can't scratch them well enough."

Without thinking about how the use of her magic might attract Circe, Sabrina pointed at the Chiapet donkey's front legs. Magic sparkles surrounded the blunt nubs at the end of them and transformed them into hands.

"Hey, thanks!" he said. He looked at her gratefully. "If you need anything while you're here, just ask for Elmer." He gave her a card and laughed. "It's been awhile since I've been able to do that. I used to be a stockbroker. Till Circe blamed me for some bad investments."

Sabrina looked at the card. It was neatly hand-lettered.

Elmer's Fruit Stand
Fruit that's good to eat,
Prices that can't be beat.
(212) 555–1234

"You have a phone?" Sabrina asked.

Elmer reached down with one of his new hands and brought up a cell phone. "It's been hard to use," he admitted. "But I won't have a problem now." He flexed his new fingers.

"I'm just surprised there are phones here."

"It's kind of hard to run a dictatorship without telecommunications these days," Elmer said. "Want me to call you a cab? It's the least I can do."

Sabrina nodded, then chatted with the Chia-pet donkey a little while longer till the Yellow Cab arrived.

"Now there's something you don't see every

day," Salem commented when the cab pulled up to the curb.

Sabrina had to agree. She also had to put Salem down because he was getting heavy.

The Yellow Cab was a hansom cab like she'd seen on the computer monitor back at Bajher's. The driver stood at the back, towering over the top of the cab and holding the reins to the four alligators.

The alligators drew Sabrina's immediate attention. Dark green on top, their yellow bellies scraped across the street as they moved, making a shush-shush-shush noise.

"Don't mistake their appearance for tardiness," the driver advised in a clipped accent that was unmistakably upper-crust British. "They're actually quite fast, you know." He stepped down and opened the door to the cab. "In you go, my dear."

Sabrina shifted her gaze again to the driver, amazed.

He was nearly nine feet tall, and looked more like a rhinoceros than a man, but there were definite human features. His face was broad, his eyes widely spaced, and two large horns sprouted up from his long nose. He wore a specially tailored three-piece gabardine suit that only made an effort at concealing his rotund figure. "And please don't step too near the steeds. They're not as disciplined as I would wish either.

Your little friend would only make a snack, I'm afraid."

"They're some of the animals—I mean, people—who forgot they were human?" Sabrina asked.

The rhinoceros gave a deep belly laugh. "Oh no, young miss, these are wild and savage alligators I captured from the sewers of this city and domesticated so that I might pursue my own entrepreneurial endeavor."

"Alligators in the sewers?" Sabrina asked.

Salem leaped up into the cab and turned back around to face her. "You knew it had to be true somewhere."

"Up you go, young miss." The rhino cab driver offered his cloven hoof, which was carefully manicured.

Sabrina took his hoof, then stepped into the cab and sat on the cushioned seat beside Salem. The hansom cab looked beautiful on the inside, all done in layered woods and brass fittings. The beauty reminded her of money, and the fare she'd be expected to pay for the ride.

"How much to the Umpire State Building?" she asked the cabdriver.

Before the driver could reply, Elmer spoke up. "Put it on my bill, Alfie. She's here looking for a friend. And she's a witch."

"A witch?" Alfie took a gold-rimmed monocle from his vest pocket and fitted it to his right eye.

"I don't think she's a bad-hearted one," Elmer

said. "She gave me hands." He showed them. "Take care of her."

"I will, mate. And believe me, I'll put the fare on your tab."

Sabrina yelled a thank-you to Elmer. The Chiapet donkey waved good-bye to her.

Alfie climbed behind the cab and took up the reins. He cracked a small whip over the heads of the alligators, who lurched into rapid action, *scrunching* across the pavement. They were off.

"Wow," Salem said, hiding in the seat, "look at the size of that one!"

Sabrina looked to the other side of the cab and watched as a huge pterodactyl glided through the air above them. The dinosaur's bloodcurdling screech echoed along West Fourth Street, but no one else on the Avenue of the Americas took any notice. *I suppose dinosaurs are pretty common.* That wasn't an especially calming thought.

"I say," Alfie said from the rear of the cab, "was that your first look at a dinosaur?"

"Outside of a movie theater and over a bowl of popcorn, yes," Sabrina replied. "I wouldn't mind if it was my last, either."

"Oh, there are plenty of the blighters," the rhinoceros man stated. "Circe generated a proper run of them for a time there."

"You realize, of course," Salem said, "that we're bite-size next to that thing."

Sabrina didn't think that was exactly true, but

it was close enough. The pterodactyl caught an updraft and glided up to the peaked roof of the United Methodist Church across from Washington Cube Fields. She'd gone to the School of the Sacred Arts on a research trip with Hilda on one of her trips to the Manhattan in the mortal realm.

"You have nothing to worry about from that beast as long as you remain within the cab," Alfie stated. "It generally has a go at the sheep living in Washington Cube Fields across the way about this time every day."

"Sheep," Sabrina said. "You mean sheep that used to be people?"

"The pterodactyl used to be a person too, you know," Alfie replied. "But he was a sailor named Howard and not an incredibly bright chap. As far as I know, he's yet to get a sheep. But he does a bang-up business out on the rivers. Of course, that's risky too, because some of the bigger dinosaurs out there are quite capable of eating him."

This isn't a very nice world Circe has built, Sabrina thought. It made her feel even worse thinking about Harvey ending up in the middle of it. She consulted the map in the cab, finding that only a few more blocks remained before they reached the Umpire State Building.

"Nervous?" Salem asked, twitching his tail as he stared out at the odd citizens living in the alternate Manhattan.

"Scared to death," Sabrina quietly admitted.

"One call over the compact flip-phone and we could be home."

"And Harvey would be stuck here. That's not going to happen." Sabrina forced her fear away. *There's a way to get around Circe. There* has *to be.*

With the binoculars she found in a pocket of her survival outfit, Sabrina stared up at the gargoyles clinging to the edge of Marcy's Department Store at the corner of Broadway and Thirty-fourth Street. She counted eleven of them, all slate gray and looking like elongated humans with massive bat wings. Sallow faces frowned beneath shaved heads, and they sat folded up on clawed feet, their taloned fingers wrapped over their bony knees.

Then she dropped the binoculars to the front of the department store and tried to spot interesting bargains. It took her only a moment to realize that all the mannequins were animals. But the giraffe-necked girl in the two-piece bikini looked great.

However, that reminded her of Libby's Valentine's Day luau. She looked to the east, down Thirty-fourth Street, and spotted the familiar lines of the Umpire State Building. The Goodbear Blimp floated lazily in the breeze in the blue sky above it.

"Hey," Salem said beside her, "it moved."

Sabrina took the binoculars down, knowing the cat wasn't talking about the blimp. "What moved?"

"One of the gargoyles." The cat raised up in the seat, placing one paw gently against the window frame.

Sabrina scanned them again. Nothing moved. "You're imagining things."

"Actually," Alfie said, "he's not. The gargoyles in this city are very much alive. In fact, they are Circe's chief spies."

Sure enough, Sabrina saw one of the gargoyles spread its wings. The batlike ridges on the underside were definitely pronounced.

"They and the guy-rillas are Circe's main troops," Alfie went on. "They're not to be trifled with. No one believes they were ever human."

"Then what were they?"

"Creatures she found in another realm, it's supposed." Alfie called out to the alligators pulling the hansom cab, urging them into a faster gait. "It has been some time since I've seen such a gathering of them."

Without warning, one of the gargoyles fell from Marcy's rooftop and plummeted toward the street.

Sabrina watched in breathless anticipation, thinking the poor creature was going to splatter against the hard surface of the street.

In the last few yards of its fall, though, the wings stretched out and seized the air. The harsh crack of wind carried to Sabrina's ears. Then the bat wings flapped, reaching far ahead of the gargoyle as it pulled itself through the air, sailing it along toward the hansom cab.

"It's spotted us!" Salem screeched. "It's coming after us!"

"Don't panic," Sabrina ordered, but her skin was crawling. She lost sight of the gargoyle as it flew behind the trees growing in Herald Square.

"Is it okay to panic if they're *all* hot on our tails?" Salem demanded.

Glancing back up at the Marcy's rooftop, Sabrina saw that all of the gargoyles had taken off from their perches. They knifed through the air, directly toward the hansom cab.

"Oh dear," Alfie said in shocked dismay, "they certainly seem to have tumbled to your presence here, dear girl."

"Then get us out of here," Sabrina suggested. *Don't panic,* she ordered herself. *Circe probably has given them orders not to hurt us. Hasn't she?*

The gargoyles swooped toward the cab, making no bones about what their target was.

"Hah-yah, you obnoxious, waddling beasts!" Alfie yelled to the alligators pulling the cab. He cracked his whip above their heads. "Pull harder!"

The cab lurched into faster speed, pulling to the inside lane and outrunning a newscart drawn by an elephant-boy. He trumpeted his snout in indignation as Alfie passed him.

"We'll never escape them in this tub," Salem declared. "We need a getaway car. Zap something up. Quick!"

Sabrina glanced at the traffic ahead of them. Thirty-fourth Street was packed with chariots, carts, and wagons. A car definitely wasn't the answer, and neither was anything aerial. She thought hard, but all she did was make her head hurt.

The cabdriver's scream was punctuated by the sound of splintering wood. When Sabrina glanced up, she saw that gargoyle claws had ripped the top of the hansom cab to pieces. Huge holes gaped and blue sky shown through them.

Two more gargoyles hit the cab, and the rooftop was gone entirely.

"Sabrina!" Salem urged.

The teenage witch glanced at the street. The alligators scurried along at a faster speed than she would have believed possible. Their claws scraping along the pavement sounded like buzz saws in a Halloween fun house.

"I'm sorry, my dear," Alfie called out, "but these poor lizards have run their best. We shan't be outrunning the gargoyles this day."

Sabrina looked at the imposing tower of the Umpire State Building ahead of her. *So close, and yet so far. Harvey, wherever you are, keep the faith. I'm not giving up.*

"Sabrina!" Salem squalled, hiding next to her.

"It's going to be okay," she told the cat. She

seized him by the fur at the scruff of his neck and shoved him into her backpack. "Sorry. And keep your head down."

"Oh, fine. The gargoyles will appreciate the gift wrapping. I'm a sausage."

Sabrina opened the door, glancing out at the traffic. She chanted quickly, visualizing what she wanted in her mind.

"Times are dangerous and I'm getting rasher,
Give me the skills and gear of a street thrasher."

Peering through the backpack, Salem screamed in terror.

Sabrina noticed the fiercesome shadow dropping around her and could almost feel the gargoyle's fetid breath against the back of her neck. She felt a tingle flood through her body, then Rollerblading gloves covered her hands and pads wrapped around her elbows and knees. A pair of high-performance Roller-Blahs replaced her flip-flops and a helmet appeared on her head in place of her floppy hat. She reached up and pulled the visor down.

"Tell me you're not going to do this," Salem cried.

"I'm not going to do this," Sabrina said, fitting herself through the open door. Then she jumped.

"You lied!" Salem wailed.

A gargoyle's claws smashed against Sabrina's helmet as she flew through the air, knocking her off balance. The street came up hard to meet her and panic filled her. She put her hands out reflexively, hoping to break her fall.

It didn't matter. Even if the fall didn't hurt her much, the huge horse-drawn wagon coming up behind her was going to run her over!

☆

Chapter 9

☆

Another tingle of magic ran through Sabrina as she fell. Suddenly she felt confident. She wasn't falling, she told herself; she was completely in control of her forward momentum. Letting her gloved hands take the impact as she tracked the wagon racing toward her, she did a handspring and landed on the Roller-Blahs racing blades. She moved fast, using the momentum she'd picked up once she dove out of the cab.

"Oh, cool," she said. "Salem, look at me." She almost danced through the traffic, giving herself over to her magic skills.

"I'd rather not," the cat replied. "And after that last loop-the-loop you just did—well, you're going to need a new backpack."

Sabrina ignored the cat and almost forgot

about the gargoyles diving down at her. It felt glorious to race along Thirty-fourth Street as if she were gravity free, totally in the zone. The vehicles on the street weren't obstacles to her now. They were opportunities waiting to be used.

She spotted the shadow of another gargoyle dive-bombing her. Bending low, she cut the skates into the pavement and skidded left, throwing out a shower of sparks. Then she leaped on to the back of one of Alfie's alligators, sliding the length of the fourteen-foot monster's back before jumping off to the left. In the on-coming lane for just an instant, she pushed hard with her feet, gaining enough speed to overtake the conventional horse-drawn traffic.

One of the gargoyles missed Sabrina when she ducked. The creature plunged headfirst into an oncoming hot dog vendor pedaling his cart in the opposite direction. Sabrina caught a glimpse of the ostrich-man abandoning his bike-cart and running away in a long-necked waddle, his eye-lashes sticking straight out in fright.

"Whoo-ha!" Salem yelped. "You go, girl!"

Sabrina cut back into the other lane to avoid the oncoming traffic. She sprinted on the blades again, building speed and passing the two lead alligators of the hansom cab.

A gargoyle screamed behind her. Glancing back briefly, she saw it coming at her, lining up its angle of attack. Turning quickly, she vaulted the curb and rolled in front of the Umpire State Building. She pointed at her Roller-Blahs.

"With matters so weighty,
ignore gravity."

Sparkles shot from her finger and enveloped the blades. Then she skated for the stone wall in front of her.

Leaping up before she reached the wall, she put her blades on the side of the Umpire State Building and rolled along, horizontal to the sidewalk and just under the gargoyle's grasping arms.

The creature smashed into the side of the building with a loud, "Ooooffff!"

Sabrina dropped back to the sidewalk and skated past the Umpire State Building just as a horde of guy-rillas in business suits came out of the main entrance. They pointed at her, then raced for the horse-drawn chariots tied up out front.

"What have you got in mind for the rest of this escape plan?" Salem asked.

"I'm working on it." Sabrina was thinking furiously. She didn't remember much other than the stores Hilda and Zelda had taken her to. She pushed hard, gaining more speed. The traffic out on Thirty-fourth Street had come to a complete halt, miring down the vehicles in the intersection of Fifth Avenue and Thirty-fourth Street.

The pursuit by the guy-rillas died as soon as it had started. Only the threat of the gargoyles remained.

Turning left and leaping up onto the sidewalk again, Sabrina zipped north on Fifth Avenue. She was getting winded, but she was holding up.

If she stayed up against the walls of the buildings, the wingspans of the gargoyles worked against them. As long as she kept up her speed, they couldn't close on her. She concentrated on keeping the blades moving, letting her magic do its stuff.

Thinking of magic reminded Sabrina that she didn't only have to act like the fleeing victim. She pointed at the lead gargoyle behind her. In an instant, a big yellow ribbon tied itself in a bow around the gargoyle's wings. The creature crashed into a wagon loaded with clothing, startling the horses.

She tied up two more of them in the same fashion, then zapped a really *huge* spiderweb across Fifth Avenue just short of the Forty-second Street intersection. She skated under the low fringe of it, knowing the gargoyles didn't have time to go over, and going under was an impossibility for them. The sound of the gargoyles smacking into the web, mixed with their angry howls, chased her down Fifth Avenue. She passed Thirty-seventh Street and came up on Thirty-sixth Street. *I'm only getting farther and farther away from Harvey.*

Desperately, she turned west on Thirty-sixth Street and skated frantically. She drew more and more attention from the local populace. Salem's head popped up from her backpack and his muzzle bounced against her shoulder.

"Any ideas?" she asked the cat.

"You're ahead of the gargoyles right now," Salem answered. "Let's keep it that way."

"I already thought of that one."

Twenty yards ahead of her, the shimmering blue-green portal Bajher had used to sneak her into Circe's world suddenly appeared. It hovered a few inches above the pavement.

"Okay," Salem said, "how about using the gateway to get out of here?"

Sabrina knew her aunts had put Bajher up to opening the gateway. She thought about it briefly, then knew she couldn't use it—not yet. No matter what their relationship turned out to be, Sabrina knew Harvey would never abandon her.

And she couldn't leave him.

She turned her blades away from the gateway, barely missing it.

"What are you doing?" Salem demanded.

"I'm going to do what I set out to do when I got here." Sabrina skated harder, cutting through the crowds of animal-people who parted before her.

A cheer broke through the crowd, and many of them waved whatever appendages they currently had in support of Sabrina's efforts. She knew they had no clue what she was doing there, but evidently any enemy of Circe's was considered a friend of theirs. She glanced over her shoulder and saw three gargoyles flapping through the air. Webbing still clung to their wings. Then she had an idea. Pointing at herself, she turned invisible.

"Good move," Salem encouraged. However, the gargoyles didn't break off their attack. "They can still hear the wheels."

Sabrina pointed again and made the bearings in the Roller-Blahs whisper-quiet. Looking over her shoulder, she noticed that the three pursuing gargoyles suddenly flew in confused patterns. "Now what? We're not going to be able to walk right into the Umpire State Building."

"I have noticed," Salem said, "even in our brief visit here, that Circe isn't exactly the favorite ruler of the city. Someone, somewhere can give us information about getting into the Umpire State Building. We just have to find that person."

"How?"

"I don't know. I don't think that person is going to be wearing a sign."

The gargoyle patrol, aided by the guy-rillas, continued their search of the area. While the gargoyles covered the airways between the tall buildings, the guy-rillas went door to door.

Sabrina, following Salem's suggestion, bladed

out to the Avenue of the Americas again, then turned north. By the time she saw Forty-second Street ahead of her, with Bryant Park on her right, Circe's pack of pursuers had grown to include creatures that looked more batlike than the gargoyles.

"Those bats won't need to see you," Salem said, "if they get their radar locked on you."

The bat-men were slightly larger than NFL linemen, with great wings that looked like leather sails as they cut through the air. They had the pug faces of bats and kept their mouths wide open as they screeched, navigating by the reflected sound waves.

"They're flying search patterns," Salem pointed out. "As fast as they're covering ground, they'll find us soon."

"They use sound waves to get around, right?" Sabrina asked.

"Right."

"So we'll go someplace noisy." She flashed past the New York Telephone Building on her left and turned on to Forty-second Street. "Times Square is over on Broadway. It's never quiet."

"Go," Salem advised. "Very fast."

Breathing hard, her muscles starting to tremble from the sustained effort, Sabrina turned left on to Forty-second Street, cutting through the stalled traffic held up by more guy-rillas.

"Evidently Circe's put out an APB on you," Salem said.

"You've been watching too much television again," Sabrina gasped. An APB was an all points bulletin.

"Maybe she has, too, but it's working because they've got traffic blocked."

"Lucky we're not traffic." Sabrina bladed down the sidewalk, slowed now by the pedestrians and bumping into some of them accidentally. She rebounded from an elephant-man and barely remained on her feet.

"This is no good," Salem pointed out. "You're leaving a trail behind."

When Sabrina glanced back, she saw that it was true. The pedestrians bumped by her had left a path behind her that pointed straight to her. Even the people ahead of her were starting to move, like a wave racing around a sports stadium. The bat-men locked on to her trail.

Using the gravity spell again, Sabrina skated straight up the side of a building fronting Times Square. The wave through the pedestrians on the sidewalk continued, and the bat-men followed it, trailed by the gargoyles and guy-rillas struggling through the stalled traffic.

Sabrina reached the rooftop of the building and rolled to a stop. She was too tired to move for a moment, but luckily none of Circe's creatures seemed to know where she was. She breathed rapidly, then coasted over to the side of the rooftop and looked down into Times Square.

Dizziness spun her vision for just a moment as she leaned out over the edge and the wind clawed at her. *No vertigo,* she told herself. *I can fly.* It worked, but barely.

Times Square, even in Circe's version of Manhattan, remained noisy. Advertisement banners clung to all the sides of buildings in the square. Surprisingly, some of them broadcast video signals. One of the huge television screens had commercials for the recent Harrison Chevy movie, and another broadcast one for Calvin Coolidge jeans. Still others in the concrete canyon advertised electronics, perfumes, restaurants, and other services.

Sabrina caught her breath, gradually cooling down as Circe's minions continued searching for her.

The noise coming from Times Square stopped the bat-men's abilities to track by sound waves. They hovered over the area restlessly, mixing in with the gargoyles.

Abruptly, the sound in Times Square died with a staticky pop. All the giant screens were cleared.

"SABRINA SPELLMAN!" Circe's voice echoed in the concrete canyon with the force of a bomb. Her image covered all the advertising screens in Times Square.

"Uh-oh," Salem said. "We could be busted."

"She can't see us," Sabrina said. "We're invisible, remember?" She stared at Circe's image.

The ancient witch was as beautiful as ever. A too-confident smile covered her face, making her look even more evil. "I know you're here, and I know *why* you're here."

The effect Circe had on the Manhattan street populace was immediate. Booing echoed up from below.

"Silence!" Circe roared. Fireworks exploded in the skies overhead, drowning out the sound of the boos and making the crowd scatter in fear. "Do not make the mistake of forgetting who I am and what power I have over you."

The booing died away.

Circe turned on the screens, getting closer. "I have what you want, little girl. And your interference here has already cost you."

The view shifted and suddenly the screens carried images of Harvey instead of Circe. He stood there, looking exactly as Sabrina remembered he had in the Westbridge High School cafeteria earlier that day.

"Sabrina can hear me?" Harvey asked hesitantly. He flicked a fingernail against the camera lens, and for a moment his finger was the only thing on the screens.

"Yes," Circe replied. "Tell her hello."

Harvey pulled his finger back and smiled the

smile Sabrina knew so well. "Cool," he said. "Hi, Sab. Isn't this dream totally rad? Well, I guess if you were here too you'd be able to answer me. And wait till you see Big Mo. Man, he is *gnarly."*

The view changed again, pulling back to include Circe and Harvey. The ancient witch wore a bronze-metallic sheath dress, which left her shoulders bare, and matching high heels. Her dark hair glittered, and her makeup brought out the impossible purple of her eyes.

"Enough, Harvey," Circe commanded.

"Sure."

The ancient witch opened her hand and blew dust over Harvey. "Now see what you've cost yourself, little girl."

The dust sparkled as it fell over Harvey. The effect was immediate. His ears and nose elongated, taking on piggy proportions and turning pink. "Hey, that tickles," he said, reaching up to touch his pig's nose. He laughed, and it sounded like a snuffle. "This is *so* cool." While he was touching his nose, his first two fingers and his second two fingers suddenly grew together in the beginning of a cloven hoof.

"Do your friend a favor, Sabrina," Circe said. "Turn yourself in before I change him more and rename him Breakfast. And I will."

Harvey was still playing with his new nose.

"Oh, Harvey," Sabrina groaned. *Why is this*

happening to me? One boring party and next I'm watching Harvey turn into a pig. This really *isn't fair.*

An ear-splitting screech ripped through the air above Sabrina. She turned, nearly falling on her Roller-Blahs despite her magically borrowed skills.

The pterodactyl launched itself from the sky, streaking straight for her. The cruel beak opened, showing gleaming sharp edges.

"Move!" Salem ordered, practically dancing in the backpack. "That thing's tracking you by scent, not sight!"

"Not good," Sabrina said. She hesitated for only a moment, watching as the heads below glanced up at the building she was on, then flung herself over the side.

The pterodactyl missed her by inches.

Sabrina fell for a short distance, then managed to swing her Roller-Blahs against the side of the building. The antigravity spell was still working and she was able to skate, but the momentum she was building up was scary. She rolled faster and faster, leaping over the windows on the side of the building that she couldn't skate around.

"Get her!" Circe screamed from the screens around Times Square. "Get her now!"

Sabrina watched the street come up to meet her. It didn't help her concentration that Salem was screaming in terror on her shoulder the whole way down. Near the bottom she leaped from the building, using her magic to slow her fall. She landed on her blades in the center of Times Square, floating over the heads of the waiting guy-rillas. The gargoyles perched atop nearby buildings and glared down while the batmen cruised beneath them.

When Sabrina touched down, she started skating again. Baying started up behind her. "What's that?"

"Hounds," Salem said.

Looking back, Sabrina glimpsed a long wagon with a caged backboard come spinning around Forty-second Street on two wheels. A team of six rainbow-colored iguana lizards running on their back legs pulled the wagon. It stopped in the middle of Times Square and a side gate opened. Humans with bloodhound features poured out of the gate and started baying their excitement. They shoved their large noses in the air, then moved unerringly in Sabrina's direction.

"They can't see me," Sabrina protested. "I'm invisible."

"They're scenting you," Salem replied. "Trained search-and-rescue dogs can air-scent, following a cone emanation projected by their target." He blinked his big yellow eyes at her. "The Discovery channel. Who says insomnia can't be a good thing?"

Sabrina focused on skating instead of on how Salem came by his knowledge. She stayed on Seventh Avenue, managing to increase her lead a little. The man-hounds kept baying but were held back by the guy-rillas who were having trouble getting through the crowd. Sabrina also noticed that most Manhattan residents were making the pursuit harder.

And they were chanting, "Sabrina! SaBRI*NA!*"

"You've got a fan club," Salem observed.

Sabrina skated up to Fiftieth Street. Her lungs burned and spots whirled in front of her eyes from the sustained effort.

Borrowed thrasher skills or not,
I can't keep this pace up.

"I've got an idea," Salem said. "Bloodhounds lose their sense of smell if they're exposed to pepper. Turn here on Fiftieth Street and find somewhere to lose yourself. Then set off a pepper bomb."

"If the man-hounds can't scent me, they can't find me. I'm invisible so I shouldn't have to hide."

"Why take chances? Next thing you know, Circe could zap out here herself."

Sabrina silently agreed. Turning north on Broadway from Fiftieth Street, she spotted the Winter Garden Theatre on the east side of the block. Aunt Zelda had taken her there to see *Cats.* It would be open to the public. *Especially the* invisible *public,* she told herself.

The pterodactyl screamed again, closer now.

"Does pepper work on pterodactyls?" Sabrina asked.

"I'm afraid the Discovery channel program didn't say," Salem replied.

"Terrific." Sabrina slid through the traffic, barely avoiding pedestrians.

> "Man-hounds are tracking me by their nose,
> erase my scent with a pepper bomb that
> blows."

She pointed.

A small explosion manifested in front of the baying man-hounds. White, smoky powder puffed out twenty feet in all directions, raining down over the man-hounds and guy-rillas. The baying changed abruptly into painful howls. The pursuit line wavered, then broke.

Hopping up onto the sidewalk, Sabrina quickly ducked into the main entrance of the Winter Garden Theatre. She rolled across the plush entryway and down into the main theater. It took a moment for her eyes to adjust to the interior lighting after being outside. When it did, she spotted the feline actors and actresses scattered across the stage.

"Cats," Sabrina said in disbelief.

"This is Circe's world," Salem said. "It makes purr-fect sense. These are my kind of people."

An itchy tingle ran through Sabrina. She dropped two inches to the ground, back in the flip-flops she'd been wearing when she'd entered the alternate Manhattan. There was no sign of her Roller-Blahs, her helmet, or any other gear. She also had the feeling she wasn't invisible anymore.

"Okay, people," a black-furred panther-person said as he walked toward the other feline cast members, "break's over. Let's get back to work."

Men and women who appeared to be stuck halfway between human and leopards, lions, tigers, Siamese cats, Manx, and calicoes shifted around the panther. Suddenly a Siamese cat-woman on the outside of the crowd pointed at Sabrina. "Hey, it's the witch girl Circe's security people have been chasing," she shrilled. The cast and production people turned to face Sabrina.

"Uh-oh," Sabrina said.

"Told you she'd put out an APB," Salem stated.

Sabrina said a quick spell again, trying to turn herself invisible. Instead, all she felt was the uncomfortable itchy tingle of a failed spell.

Her magic was gone!

The cast of *Cats* closed on her, their excited voices all mixing together.

Sabrina tried to retreat, but the door she'd come through was suddenly filled by the bulk of a cleaning man with a lion's mane around his neck and shoulders. He bared his fangs and growled a warning deep in his throat.

"Don't try to run, little girl, and you won't get hurt!"

Salem erupted from the backpack and landed on a nearby seat back. "Back off, Shaggy," the cat ordered. He swiped a paw full of extended claws at the lion-man's nose.

The lion-man drew back with a startled yelp. He emptied the trash can he was carrying, dumping the contents on to the floor. Then he advanced on Salem cautiously. "You're out of your weight class, small fry."

Sabrina pointed at the man, hoping to knock him off balance. The itchy tingle filled her finger. Nothing happened. "Salem, my magic's not working."

"Now you tell me." Salem leaped over the lion-man's hand as he swatted at Salem, and landed on the trash container. From there he jumped on the lion-man's head and covered the man's eyes with his paws. Frightened, the lion-man ran into a wall and knocked himself down. Salem leaped to safety.

Sabrina wheeled on the cast members, angry and scared at the same time. But mostly she couldn't believe they were trying to catch her. "Are you people crazy? Or do you like living here with Circe?"

The cast members halted, advancing for a moment. "At least we're living," a leopard-woman stated.

"Yeah," the panther-director added. "And at

least we have hands. Not like those poor schmucks down in Chiatown."

"I could be your last hope here," Sabrina said. "I came into this world hoping to save a friend of mine. I'm a witch."

The *Cats* cast members looked to their director. He shook his head. "If you have to beg us not to capture you, how are you going to stand up against Circe?" the director asked.

Sabrina was stumped. She looked at Salem, who was still fending off the lion-man's advances. "You can jump in here any minute to help me."

Salem flicked his tail hypnotically. "I'm kind of busy here."

Sabrina pointed her finger.

The cast members cowered, diving behind the high-backed seats. Except for the director. "Her magic's not working," he said. "Circe has shorted her out. Otherwise she'd have already done something to get away." He walked toward her, gradually joined by the other cast members.

Sabrina glanced around. There was nowhere to run. Then a voice said, "This way!"

☆

Chapter 10

☆

Sabrina glanced up at the speaker.

He stepped out of the shadows, only a few inches taller than she was and as animallike as the other cast members of *Cats*. His head had the regal contours and coloring of a Bengal tiger, orange-red and white striped. His eyes were dark and warm brown. He wore khaki slacks and a black turtleneck. He didn't wear shoes because his feet resembled paws more than any human foot. No way would Guccis or Doc Martens cover those.

In his face, though, Sabrina saw youth and compassion. A gold hoop dangled from his tufted left ear, giving him a pirate appearance.

"Roland!" the panther-man director bellowed. "What do you think you're doing?"

The Bengal tiger-man spoke with an accent

that thrilled Sabrina. It sounded French, definitely European, but it was different from what she would have believed.

"I was a knight in Charlemagne's court, and was raised on honor and courage," Roland responded. "There is no other way that I may act." He put those liquid eyes on Sabrina again. "It's time to go, *mam'selle.*"

"Stop her, Leo," Morely, the panther director, ordered.

The lion-man stepped forward, and Roland moved to intercept him, reaching out for the broom that was leaning against the wall behind a nearby seat. Holding up one end, he stomped on the handle, neatly breaking the broom section away. He raised the broken haft in one hand and swung it like a sword, connecting with Leo's big paws.

The swats must have stung, Sabrina guessed, because the big lion-man yelped in pain and surprise.

Morely and the cast rushed forward, only Roland's broken mop handle was there to stop them. The young tiger-man rapped the director on the nose and caused Morely to draw back. The wave of approaching *Cats* cast members broke across Morely's back.

"Stand back," Roland said in a powerful voice, holding the mop handle poised. "I have no wish to harm any of you. You've been good to me. But I'll not see this young woman roughly handled while I may yet take up arms to protect her. And I'll not dishonor my liege's memory by failing to do that which he bade me do when he bestowed upon me a royal knighthood."

"Rowwrrr," one of the leopard-women growled appreciatively. A smile curved her spotted lips. "Who would have guessed Roland had such fire within him, Morely? Look at that expression. So serious, so fierce. If only Jervis could capture that on the stage."

"Keep that in mind," Morely grumped, "when Circe finds out we let them get away."

Roland kept the mop handle at the *en garde* position. *"Mam'selle,* would you do me the honor of trusting me so that I may aid in your escape?"

Sabrina loved listening to the young tiger-man speak. She loved it so much, in fact, that she forgot she'd been asked a question. For a moment. The theatrical cast members spreading out around them quickly reminded her of the trouble she was in. "We gotta go," she agreed.

"Eloquently put, *mam'selle.* I urge you to make haste. Allow me, and please excuse the uninvited familiarity our situation bids me show you." Roland grabbed Sabrina's hand and pulled her toward an exit on the far side of the room.

Sabrina ran, matching the tiger-man's pace, but her legs were quivering and tired from her skating. She pointed at herself, but her magic failed her once again. *If only my magic still worked, I could refresh myself. I'm definitely not going to be much help in the escape department.* Salem matched their pace easily.

"Where are we going?" Sabrina asked. "I'm only asking because going outside isn't a really cool idea right now."

"I know," Roland responded. "There is another way." He led her through the side exit and down a hallway past other doors. He kept the mop handle in hand. "The stock room has an exit to the underground sewers. I know because I helped build it."

"Sewers?" Sabrina repeated. *Eeewwww! I don't need no stinking sewers!*

Roland released her hand long enough to open a side door at the end of the hallway. "I'm sorry, *mam'selle,* to subject your delicate sensitivities to such extremes, but they are necessary."

"It's okay," Sabrina replied.

"She's not that sensitive," Salem put in.

Roland glanced down at the cat. "Are you sure that's not an evil creature?"

"Most of the time." Sabrina followed the young tiger-man into the stockroom, then watched as he pushed crates aside to lift a section of the floor. A tunnel appeared, and the stench was strong enough to peel fingernail polish.

"Oh, man," Sabrina groaned.

"I know," Roland said, "and I apologize. But

those people will have Circe's guy-rillas down on you in moments. She's trained them over the years to be self-serving."

"I got that impression." Sabrina turned to Salem. "You can see in the dark. Why don't you go first?"

"Cats seeing in the dark is a myth," Salem insisted. He turned his eyes on her. "And don't you remember Alfie saying where he had captured those alligators that pulled the yellow cab?"

"There are very few alligators," Roland said. He barred the door with the mop handle just as hesitant feet sounded out in the hallway.

"All it takes is one," Salem said.

"I'll handle them. Please go." Roland pushed aside a box on the top shelf and seized a fuel oil bull's-eye lantern.

Sabrina went down a ladder built into the side of the tunnel. The icky smell grew even worse, until she could barely breathe. But she went, and Salem followed.

"I made this tunnel not long after Circe moved us here." Roland had the lead, holding the bull's-eye lantern high. The strong yellow beam carved a path through the sewer tunnel.

Sabrina had found that by breathing shallowly the stink wasn't quite so bad. "Why?"

"Part of an escape plan that has never quite come to fruition, *mam'selle.*"

"You're really a knight?" Sabrina tried to ignore the slimy walls and the sound of the lapping water to her left.

"Oui, mam'selle, and given the title by Charlemagne himself." Roland sounded proud.

Sabrina tried to remember her history classes, but things that happened much past the last fashion change had never really been of much interest to her. "Charlemagne was the king of someplace, wasn't he?"

Roland smiled, and Sabrina decided that she liked the expression. The tiger look suited him. Especially now that he had belted a sword around his narrow hips and pulled on a chain mail shirt with a fierce tiger crest embroidered on a yellow half-shirt.

"Charlemagne was *my* king, *mam'selle,"* Roland answered. "And never did a finer king ever sit a throne."

"I guess you've been away from the mortal world for a long time."

"Hundreds of years, *mam'selle."*

"So why help me?"

"Because you need it." Roland ducked under a supporting arch on the ceiling and took a new tunnel off the one they followed. "Why did you come after your friend? Harvey, is that his name?"

"Harvey," Sabrina agreed. "I came after him because I know he would have come after me if I needed his help."

"He sounds like a good friend."

"The best." Sabrina ducked under the arch too, covering her head so the green goop hanging off it wouldn't touch her hair.

"Perhaps more, *mam'selle?* An affair of the heart?"

"Hey, Lancelot," Salem growled from between them, "you're getting kind of personal, aren't you?"

Roland stopped and bowed, holding on to the sword hilt with his free hand. "A thousand pardons, *mam'selle,* if I have offended you. I did not mean to pry, but your situation is unique here in this land, and your feelings do have a bearing on what we can and must do."

"My feelings?" Sabrina echoed.

"But of course," Roland answered. "Have you heard the tale of Odysseus, who was the first to escape Circe's island all those years ago?"

"Yes. He was aided by Hermes who gave him some kind of root or herb." Sabrina was surprised she remembered the story.

Roland paused a moment to boot a curious alligator in the snout. The big lizard lost interest and sank back into the water. "Then the legends have survived in the mortal realm. Good."

"You said Odysseus was the first." Sabrina edged cautiously around the area where the alligator disappeared. "There were others?"

"Oui," Roland answered. "But not for a long time, and less than a handful of them. Solly was

the last to come the closest. It was his near-escape that caused Circe to build this place. I sought him out when I found out about him. And it was he who told me that it would require a witch of good heart to allow us to escape."

"Solly's still here though, right?" Salem asked.

"*Oui.* Circe changed him into a"—he paused at a loss for words—"a *troll.* I guess that would be the closest approximation you would know. He lives near the Lincoln Tunnel, which is where we are headed."

"If he's still there, then maybe old Solly doesn't have all the answers," the cat stated.

"If he doesn't," Roland replied, "no one does."

Sabrina continued following the young tiger-man through the darkness, winding through the labyrinth of tunnels. She'd tried the compact cell phone earlier, but she hadn't been able to reach her aunts or Bajher. For the moment she had no choice but to go with Roland.

She had to wonder how much of a pig Circe had made of Harvey.

Solly really did live beside the Lincoln Tunnel. Sabrina gratefully followed Roland into fresh air and stood on the bank of the Hudson River. Gray fog masked the other bank, and just looking in that direction made Sabrina feel a chill.

"Nothing lives out there," Roland said as he

guided them along the bank. Weeds had grown up between broken sections of concrete, some of them four- and five-feet tall.

Without warning, a dinosaur's head broke the surface of the Hudson River. Sabrina guessed that it was twenty- or thirty-feet long and at least half that across. The head sat on a spindly neck. It bellowed mournfully.

"I feel especially sorry for the dinosaurs," Roland said softly. "Circe was more angry with those people than most and tampered with their memories when she changed them. Still, though, some of them, from time to time, do remember what it was like to be human."

The grade grew steeper. Roland had no problems with it on his tiger's feet, but Sabrina nearly fell. He offered her a furry hand and she took it, climbing to the top of a hill and watching the huge bulk of the Lincoln Tunnel grow closer overhead.

"Why's everything breaking up here?" Salem asked as he bounded through the weeds.

"Solly thinks it's because Circe's magic that created this island is beginning to fragment," Roland answered. "She's a very selfish witch. She created this place as our prison, but she doesn't keep it up. Solly believes that it may all disappear one day—us with it."

"That's terrible," Sabrina said.

The young tiger-man nodded. "And we who

are trapped here can't do anything about it, *mam'selle.* That's why what you're able to do is so important."

But what if I can't do anything? Sabrina thought. *My magic is gone. Don't you understand that?* But she didn't want to say anything out loud because she was depending on her magic to save Harvey as well.

Roland led her to a clearing near the Lincoln Tunnel. "Solly, I've brought a visitor."

A huge creature moved out of the shadows of the tunnel. He was covered in matted gray fur, and two long and warped ebony horns jutted up from his forehead. His face was decidedly goat-like, long and narrow, with a wiry tuft of hair on his bony chin. He moved upright on his back legs but with effort, using a gnarled tree limb to aid him.

"Who?" Solly asked in a voice that resembled a bleat.

"Her name is Sabrina Spellman. She's a witch."

Solly tilted his head, studying Sabrina. "The one Circe's guy-rillas search for."

"Oui." Roland grinned at Sabrina. "Solly has spies everywhere."

The troll's home was created of braided rushes and weeds from the riverbank. He'd constructed a small hut that Sabrina had to admit looked quite homey.

"Is it true that Circe has taken your magic?" Solly asked.

"Not taken it," Sabrina corrected. "But she has managed to block it. Somehow."

"You can't lift this spell from yourself?"

"No. I have a book at home, *The Discovery of Magic.* If I had it, maybe it would help."

"You came here by yourself?"

Quickly Sabrina explained about her aunts and Bajher. She held up the compact. "I haven't been able to contact them yet."

Solly rummaged in the matted fur covering his chest and took off a necklace. A glowing green stone hung from it. "Try holding this next to it. It is a chip from the First Stone. It holds a bit of magic in it."

Sabrina took the necklace and felt the magic tingling in the stone. She held it against her compact and flipped it open. The mirror cleared of her reflection, revealing Bajher's computer cave. Her aunts stared back at her worriedly.

"Sabrina, are you all right?" Zelda asked.

"So far," Sabrina answered. She explained about her powers and told them how Circe was turning Harvey into a pig.

"We can't help you yet," Hilda said, her face filled with anxiety. "We shouldn't have let you go over there."

"What about the Witches' Council?" Sabrina asked.

"So far they're refusing to take part in anything. Some of them feel you violated Circe's space by going over there."

"She took Harvey. I couldn't just let her do that."

"Circe's taken other mortals over the years. The council is like any other national body, sweetheart, and isn't going to get involved."

"That's stupid," Sabrina said angrily.

"If they involved themselves too deeply, they wouldn't be a democratic entity," Hilda pointed out. "They'd only be a step away from a full-blown dictatorship. You know that."

Sabrina nodded. The Witches' Council wasn't set up to police the entire witch populace. And it shouldn't have to. *But Circe is* so *bad.*

The communications connection over the compact became staticky.

"You don't have much time," Solly bleated. "There's not much magic in that stone. I'd hoped you'd at least be able to return to your friends."

"Bajher's working on a new spellgram for the computer," Zelda said. "I'm helping where I can. We're hoping to open another gateway in the next couple of hours."

"Hurry," Sabrina said. "Otherwise you may only bring Sabrina the Chiapet home."

The static increased and wiped out her aunts' puzzled expressions. Then she was staring at her own reflection again. She handed the necklace back to Solly.

"I'm sorry," the troll said, slipping the necklace back on. "Circe is a most unkind witch. I'm afraid she won't be easy on you. But you may be able to hide from her for a time. You do miss your humanity."

"Thank you," Sabrina told him.

"You guys sound like a bunch of losers," Salem exploded in indignation.

All of them turned to the cat.

"You just told us in the tunnels that Solly here knew a lot about escaping from this world," Salem said. "And you asked Sabrina about her feelings concerning Harvey. You even brought up Odysseus's escape from Circe. There was a reason for that, so let's hear it."

Roland glanced at Solly uncertainly.

"It is a small chance at best," the troll said after a moment.

"Even if I don't have my powers?" Sabrina asked.

Solly nodded. "Even so. Your powers may be blocked, but you're still a witch. That matters."

"I'm only half-witch," she pointed out.

"That should be enough," Solly replied.

Salem sat on his haunches. "So give us the details. I don't exactly like the idea of working in the blind."

"We'll tell you on the way," Roland said.

"On the way?" Salem opened his eyes wide. "Look, I don't like operating by the seat of my pants."

"This from the master planner who failed at taking over the world," Sabrina said. But a tingle of fear ran through her as well.

"Hey," Salem argued, "I've got about seventy more years as a cat. That's all. And I don't want that jinxed."

Solly walked back into his grass hut and returned with a long cape that he pulled over his shoulders.

"Oh great," Salem said, "and we're being led by an old goat who thinks he's a superhero."

Roland paused by Sabrina. "Your cat is not an overly affectionate pet, is he?"

"It's way past dinnertime, pal," Salem grumped.

The young tiger-man chose to ignore the cat. "Solly is old," he told Sabrina. "He gets cold easily these days. Circe's magic hasn't prevented him from aging. He's older than anyone I've ever met. It is very hard for him to take on this journey."

"I understand."

"If we don't succeed, I doubt very much that he'll return here."

Sabrina didn't know what to say to that. *If we fail, I don't think any of us will be returning anywhere real soon.*

* * *

They followed the sewers back under Manhattan. Roland checked marks inscribed on the walls at different junctures, choosing alternate paths through the tunnels. Twice, they stopped and hid as guy-rilla patrols walked through the sewers searching for them.

"Odysseus was the first to escape Circe's clutches," Solly whispered as they moved along. "He did it with Hermes' help, and because of one thing that even Circe's magic couldn't negate. He loved his wife very much and wanted to get home to her. Circe could not bind that love.

"Love will always find a way," Solly continued. "It is the truest magic of them all. It makes strong men weak, and weak men strong. It blinds, and it makes things clear. It deafens, and it makes the smallest word speak volumes of thoughts."

"But other people live here," Sabrina said. "They must have loved others too."

"They," Roland pointed out, "are not witches. Nor has Hermes seen fit to help anyone here."

"Maybe we are hidden too far away for Hermes to find us." Solly used his cane to get past a slippery area.

Roland stopped, examining the latest marks on the wall. Then he shone the bull's-eye lantern up an access tunnel through the roof. "We're here."

Sabrina stepped closer, looking up the tunnel at the ladder on the side.

"Here where?" Salem asked.

Sabrina thought she knew even before Roland answered.

"Under the Umpire State Building," the young tiger-man answered.

"Now who," Salem asked, "had this bright idea?"

Chapter 11

I fear I must rest."

Sabrina looked down at Solly the troll. She was just behind Roland and Salem as they were making their way up the steep, narrow stairs leading up into the heart of the Umpire State Building.

The troll wheezed, straining to regain his breath. "Go on without me."

"I'll not leave you, old friend." Roland went back down the steps and drew one of Solly's arms across his shoulders. The young tiger-man was dwarfed by the troll's bulk. Still, Roland managed to start them both up the stairs. But they were only on the seventh floor of the building, staying hidden within a darkened emergency stairwell that Roland knew hadn't been used in years. There were still seventy-nine floors to go.

"They'll never make it," Salem said, sitting on the next landing.

"No," Sabrina agreed. She looked at the thin carpet the cat was sitting on, then at the leaf and wire bracelet on her wrist. It was the only thing that protected her from the full fury of Circe's magic. She felt the tingle of magic within the bracelet. "At least, they're not going to make it without my help."

She took the bracelet off and concentrated on it. One of the spells she had learned in *The Discovery of Magic* book had been how to put her magic into things and later pull it out. Circe had blocked her magic, but maybe she hadn't cut off access to other magics.

After a moment Sabrina felt the magic stirring in the bracelet and was certain she could use it. She left it there for a moment and turned to Roland. "Can you cut this carpet free?"

"*Oui,* but why?"

"I think I can use it."

"Magic?" Solly asked. "But you should save it."

"This magic can't be saved," Sabrina said. "And it's not enough to do anything to Circe. But it can help us now."

Roland cut the section of carpet free with his sword.

"Everybody sit in the middle," Sabrina instructed. Once everyone was seated, she drained the magic from the bracelet and used it in her spell.

"No more tired sighs,
let this carpet become one that flies."

Immediately the carpet levitated and a small control knob jutted up in front of Sabrina. She moved it and found the carpet was sensitive. "Hang on," she said, starting them up the next flight of stairs. "Wish I'd thought to put headlights on this thing."

Roland held the lantern forward so she could see. "What was the bracelet?" the young tiger-man asked.

"Nothing," Sabrina replied, feeling the deadweight of it against her wrist.

"It was her last defense," Solly said. "Now she is as vulnerable as we are."

"That's true, *mam'selle?"* Roland asked.

"Yeah," Sabrina said as she kept the carpet floating upward. "But we wouldn't have made it any other way."

"What are we looking for?" Salem asked in a whisper.

Sabrina piloted the flying carpet into the landing on the eighty-sixth floor. It was still dark, and Roland's lantern had been sputtering for the last ten floors.

"The First Stone," Solly replied. "Circe commanded me to help her set it in this world. When she raised this Manhattan, it was stored on this floor of this building."

"What's so important about it?" Sabrina asked.

"It is that which binds all things here," Solly answered. "The centerpiece of Circe's particular magics here. It can only be handled by a witch."

Sabrina halted the flying carpet, perplexed by the maze of corridors that spread out in both directions. She was amazed that Circe hadn't found out they were in the building. But the ancient witch was very confident in her abilities as well.

"Which way?" she asked.

Solly pointed.

They got off the carpet and Sabrina rolled it up, using cord Roland provided to hang it over her shoulder. They went in the direction Solly led them.

Roland quietly picked the lock on the hidden door that barred them from the room where Solly said the First Stone was kept.

Sabrina watched as the door swung open and the young tiger-man stepped inside. On the inside of the large room, the door was actually part of the wall.

The room turned out to be a circular amphitheater fifty feet high. It was filled with statues of

Circe, ranging from a few inches tall to one thirty feet in height. Frescoes covered the walls, all depicting scenes from the legends of Circe.

Sabrina was captivated by their savage beauty. Her eyes roved along the scenes, able to see them because of the light coming in from the glass dome built into the ceiling.

"Mam'selle," Roland called in a whisper. "We must hurry."

"Sure," Sabrina replied, pulling herself away from the artwork. "Sorry." She spotted Salem trotting beside Solly, his tail switching hypnotically, and she hurried to catch up to her companions.

Solly stood in front of a stone mosaic free-standing in the center of the room. Thousands of colored stones created the picture. Circe's image was undeniable. The ancient witch, looking much like the teenager that Sabrina knew, stood on a balcony created by the branches of a giant tree. A forest spread out before her, and hundreds of animals bent down in obvious subjugation. Beyond them were men and women.

"It's here," Solly said, pointing at the mosaic.

"The First Stone?" Sabrina asked.

The troll nodded. "She had this mosaic built as a testament to her power—and to hide the First Stone."

Sabrina stretched a hand toward the mosaic. She felt the magic inherent in the artwork. It was so strong, like nothing she'd ever felt before. It made the hollow inside her, where her magic had been, even more apparent. "Which one?"

"There." Solly pointed at one of the plain green stones making up the forest floor. "The First Stone, that power which binds this world together, and which makes prisoners of those who live here."

"What do I need to do?" Sabrina asked.

"Remove it from the mosaic and break the enchantment," the troll replied.

"That's all?" Sabrina asked. "I was looking more for guidance on how to do something like that."

Solly shook his head. "I don't know, child. I don't even know that it can be done. But I know only a witch may touch it."

Summoning her courage, Sabrina reached for the First Stone. An electric charge rushed through her fingers when she touched it. She pried at it, feeling it move slightly, but it didn't come free.

Then an electrical current snapped at her, causing her to pull her hand back. "I can't," she told Solly.

"You must," the troll replied. Pain and anxiety filled his eyes. "There is no other way. All I know is locked up in that stone."

"It's not enough!" a harsh voice declared.

Sabrina spun as lights filled the darkened room, chasing the shadows away. Her eyes fixed on Circe. The ancient witch led a band of guy-rillas toward her.

Circe's eyes flicked toward Solly. "You disappoint me, old troll. I thought you'd learned the error of your ways."

"Never," Solly replied angrily. "Not as long as I remember what freedom was."

"I gave you freedom," Circe replied. "You have your little grass hut." She turned her gaze back to Sabrina. "And you, little girl, you should have learned not to bother me. Look at what it's already cost you." She snapped her fingers.

Three guy-rillas came from the back of the crowd, pushing Harvey in front of them. His transformation had gone even further than when Sabrina had last seen him. Harvey's face was nearly all pig now, heavy jowls and furry skin. His clothing stretched tight against his big belly, but his sleeves hung long on his shortened piggy arms.

"Harvey," Sabrina cried out.

"Hey, don't worry about it, Sab," Harvey grunted. He oinked a few times for good measure. "This is really the coolest dream I've ever had."

Except it's not a dream, Harvey. Sabrina's heart ached. She just wanted to sit down and cry.

Circe approached Sabrina, waving her guy-rilla guards back into place. "What have we here, little girl?" She touched the leaf and wire bracelet. "You've even come here without your precious little trinket's power. How very charming for me."

"Look," Sabrina said, "you've got me here. That's what you wanted. So why don't you just turn Harvey back and send him back to the mortal realm? You never wanted him."

Circe looked back at Harvey. "I find I have developed a certain *fondness* for him after today." She looked deep into Sabrina's eyes. "I think I'll keep him here, if only to torment you more properly. And maybe one day I'll entertain you with—*breakfast.*" She laughed and the sound filled the large amphitheater.

Sabrina had never felt more helpless, even during her parents' divorce. Harvey stood there, hunched over, having trouble just standing.

Solly grabbed her arm. "Don't give up, Sabrina. You can't."

"Shut up, you old fool," Circe snapped. "The little girl's beaten and she knows it."

The troll ignored her. "Sabrina, her magic may be stronger than yours, but you've known something much stronger than she ever has."

Circe pointed and a steel collar appeared around the troll's mouth.

It was too late. Sabrina knew what the old troll had been talking about. She had come there because of her love for Harvey, because she cared so much about him—because she knew in her heart that he felt the same way about her.

But was it the true love that kept a romance alive through troubles and years?

She didn't know, and the uncertainty tore at her. A romantic chemistry existed between them, a spark at least, but nothing like the love Odysseus must have felt for his wife.

Or was it?

Love was love. She loved her mother and father. She loved her aunts. She loved Salem.

And one thing she was *certain* of regarding Harvey Kinkle, she did love him too. No matter where romance took her, even if it took her away from him, she knew a part of her would always love him—truly, madly, and deeply.

She turned back to the mosaic, aware that Circe was turning her attention back to her. "Roland," Sabrina called out.

"At your service, *mam'selle.*"

"I need a moment."

The young tiger-man leaped into action, baring his long sword and scaring the guy-rillas back. Even Circe paused a beat. Then the ancient witch recovered, throwing a hand toward Sabrina. Before she could utter whatever spell she chose, Salem sailed through the air and landed on her head, causing her to screech in panic.

Sabrina focused on the mosaic, on the First Stone. On her love for Harvey. And she let her heart find its way through the tangle of spells Circe had woven over the mosaic. Her fingers dug at the First Stone, pulling it free of the stone tablet. When she had it in her hand, she turned to the ancient witch.

"No one," Sabrina said as she held the First Stone where Circe could see it, "is going to stay here any more. We're all going home." She felt her magic returning, overpowering whatever spell Circe had placed on her. "And Harvey isn't going to be a pig *any*more."

Magic sparkles shot from Sabrina's hand when the First Stone evaporated and quickly spread over Harvey, returning him to human form.

"Way to go, Sab," Harvey congratulated her. "Wait till I tell you how fab you were in my dream when I see you again."

The magic sparkles continued swirling, changing Roland into a young red-haired knight with flashing emerald eyes. His sword kept all the guyrillas at bay. Solly became an aged man with gray hair dressed in monk's robes. Salem dashed into the sparkles, but he remained a cat, crying plaintively. The sparkles continued whirling around, shattering the glass dome overhead and shooting out in all directions.

"You haven't won, little girl!" Circe shouted.

Sabrina held her gaze on the woman. "You're *so* over."

Sudden tremors shivered through the Umpire State Building, coming from below.

"Not yet," Circe said.

"Cool," Harvey said, dodging one of the falling statues, "you're going to get to see Big Mo, Sab."

Sabrina definitely didn't have a good feeling about meeting someone named Big Mo. "Who's Big Mo?"

Before Harvey could answer, a section of wall to their left shattered inward, leaving a hole forty feet high. The big ape that forced its way through the hole had to bend over to make it.

"Rrrrooowwwwlllll!" the ape roared.

"Big Mo," Harvey said, nodding and smiling. "This is a really cool dream, Sab. I wish you could be here. But I'll tell you all about it."

"Maybe you'll tell me how we got away," Sabrina said.

"Hey, I'm just hanging, waiting to see what happens next," Harvey replied. "Something will come up."

Up! That's the answer, Sabrina thought. She peered up through the broken glass dome in the ceiling, spotting the umpire's statue that had given the building its name.

The Goodbear blimp hovered just beyond the statue.

"Get them, Big Mo!" Circe ordered the ape.

It growled and lumbered toward Sabrina and Harvey. The teenage witch pulled the carpet from her shoulder. Maybe her magic was still wonky from being in Circe's kingdom, but the carpet held magic from the bracelet. "Everybody get on the carpet," she directed.

Solly, Salem, and Roland joined her on it at once. The guy-rillas closed in immediately, then backed away as Big Mo came closer. His thundering footsteps shook the whole floor.

Harvey remained where he was, totally enraptured by everything going on. "Wow."

Sabrina stood briefly and grabbed him, dragging him onto the carpet.

"Now what?" Harvey asked, lying down among them.

"Gotta go," Sabrina said, taking control of the flying carpet. With Harvey's additional weight, the carpet didn't float or handle nearly as well. They sailed upward, through the dome, and Big Mo's hand closed bare inches from the trailing fringe of the carpet.

"Bon chance favors us, *mam'selle,"* Roland said, grinning. "But where are we going?"

"To the Goodbear blimp," Sabrina replied. "I don't know how much longer the magic powering the flying carpet is going to last." She already felt it wavering, sputtering beneath them. Still, it lasted long enough to get them to the blimp.

Roland broke the lock on the gondola door and they clambered aboard with Big Mo hot on their heels. The sixty-foot ape crawled through the broken dome of the Umpire State Building,

Circe sitting on his shoulder and screaming orders to get them. Big Mo reached for the Goodbear blimp.

"The mooring rope!" Salem cried out. "It's holding us to the building!"

Sabrina saw that it was true. The thick rope tied them to the mooring ring on top of the building. She pointed, but her magic wasn't back.

"I'll get it," Roland said, moving into the doorway. But before the young knight could slash at the mooring rope with his sword, Big Mo punched the Goodbear blimp.

Everyone in the gondola spilled across the control room. Roland tried to get to his feet and reach for his sword. A pained grimace filled his handsome face as his injured leg slid out from under him.

"I've got it," Harvey said. "Let me have the sword."

"No," Sabrina said, afraid for him.

"Are you kidding?" Salem growled. "Give him the sword or Bongo down there is going to make a *piñata* out of us."

Roland hesitated only a moment. The gondola still swung wildly. He glanced at her. "We have no choice, *mam'selle.*" He surrendered the sword to Harvey. "Swing truly and with your heart, friend Harvey."

"Yeah. Sure." He smiled at Sabrina. "I really

like it when I get to be the hero in my dreams." He ran to the doorway, making his way through the swinging gondola, then swung at the thick mooring rope.

Sabrina followed him, watching as the rope parted and Big Mo swung another mighty blow. The gondola shivered and floated up just as Harvey tumbled out through the door.

"Harvey!" Sabrina screamed. Without hesitation, she threw herself through the door and dragged the flying carpet after her. During the fall as she and Harvey raced toward the street, she climbed on top of the flying carpet and took control of it.

Throwing the carpet into a power dive, she swooped under Harvey and caught him. "I've come a long way to make sure you're safe and sound, Harvey Kinkle," she told him as he started laughing and telling her how cool the whole experience was, "and you're not going to louse that up." She guided them back to the Goodbear blimp's gondola, tracking smoothly under the zeppelin bear's smile.

Together they watched the magic sparkles spread out over the alternate Manhattan, changing everything.

"You've done it, dear girl," Solly said, coming up to clap Sabrina on the shoulder.

"I guess I have," Sabrina said. "But I couldn't have done it without you guys."

Salem prowled through the gondola as they

floated. "Don't they serve meals on these flights?"

"I don't think we'll have time," Sabrina said when she saw the familiar shimmering blue green gateway open in the air before them. It was time to go home.

☆

Chapter 12

☆

Aren't you interested in what happened to Circe?"

Sabrina sat at the kitchen table in the Spellman home and finished wrapping the heart-shaped box of candy she'd gotten for Harvey. *Not that I'll be needing it,* she thought. It was Valentine's Day, and though Harvey hadn't said anything, she fully expected him to go to Libby Chessler's Hawaiian luau.

"Not really," Sabrina told Hilda, putting her gift to one side. It depressed her even more that her gift wasn't more inspired. *How lame can you get, giving a candy heart for Valentine's Day?* Of course, there was the fact that her relationship with Harvey wasn't quite a romance. But then, nobody said it wasn't either.

Hilda stood in the kitchen pointing up strawberry tarts. She and Zelda were having a few guests over later. "Why not?" Hilda asked.

"Okay," Sabrina said, "tell me what happened to Circe." She already knew from Roland and Solly that the alternate Manhattan had disappeared and all the people Circe had captured over the years had gone back to their own time periods and realms with only a few days missing from their lives. For most of them, like Harvey Kinkle, the time spent in Circe's Manhattan would only be remembered as a dream.

"I thought you'd want to know," Hilda said, putting another tray of tarts in the refrigerator. "Zelda and I represented you at the Witches' Council. They voted unanimously to put her on probation. Any major magic she uses is going to have to be okayed by the council."

Salem leaped to the top of the kitchen counter and shook his head. "Everything she did, and no one turned *her* into a cat."

Hilda shot him a reproachful look. "Although a certain someone who shall remain nameless did start up a petition to have that done."

"Hey," Salem said, "I happen to think she would have made a very cute cat. Being alone on Valentine's Day is kind of rough, you know."

"Actually," Hilda said, "the only reason the council didn't turn Circe into some kind of animal was so she wouldn't have any common ground with Salem. They decided that together the two of them would be a little too dangerous."

"Hrummph," the cat said.

Zelda entered the room and surveyed the tarts Hilda was pointing up. "Sabrina, aren't you still going to the Slicery tonight?"

"Yes."

"You don't really sound enthusiastic."

"I'm not," Sabrina admitted.

"Isn't Harvey going to be there?"

"I don't know," Sabrina answered. "He wasn't *sure* when I phoned him this morning."

The aunts looked at each other.

"Hey, look," Sabrina said, "I know you guys have a party planned, so I'll just be on my way."

"You don't have to go," Hilda protested.

"Actually," Sabrina said, "if I'm going to be miserable on Valentine's Day, I'd rather be miserable at the Slicery tonight. Valerie will probably be there, and misery loves company."

"There are parties going on in the Other Realm tonight," Zelda said. "I'm sure you'd be welcome."

My life happens to be here, Sabrina thought. "It's okay. Have fun." She zapped herself into her coat, scarf, and mittens and walked outside. She briefly considered zapping herself to the Slicery, but the night sky was clear and she thought she could use the time alone. Maybe the cold walk would numb all the unhappiness inside her.

The past week had been confusing. Libby had made a bigger deal of her luau than anyone expected, and Harvey had been gone most of the time they usually spent together before *and* after school. It had bothered her that she didn't know where he was. Their relationship was so confusing.

But it hadn't seemed that way back in the other Manhattan. She'd been certain how she felt there. *Why hadn't that certainty come back into the mortal realm with her?*

She sighed and watched her gray plume of breath gust out in front of her.

"Sab! Hey, Sab, wait up!"

She stopped and turned around, spotting Harvey coming toward her at a lope.

"Hey," he said when he fell into step beside her, "sorry I'm late."

"You did tell me you weren't *sure* if you could make it," Sabrina reminded with a tone she really didn't intend to use. "You've been gone a lot lately. I thought you'd probably go to Libby's luau."

"There's not going to be a luau. Libby and a half-dozen cheerleaders ended up getting burned in tanning beds as a result of a competition to see who could get the darkest quickest, so the party was called off."

"I didn't know that." But the idea of a half-baked Libby was comforting.

"You've kind of been off in your own world," Harvey said.

At least it wasn't someone else's, Sabrina thought.

"I was going to tell you after I heard," Harvey said, "but I didn't see you again."

"I know," Sabrina replied. "You've been busy."

"I have," Harvey said, "but I really wanted to get this for you." He took a small gift-wrapped box from his pocket. "Money's been kind of scarce since Christmas, but I spent the mornings and afternoons shoveling snow for businesses, like the theater, and private homes for the last few weeks and picked up a few extra bucks. Thanks again for that lotion, because it really helped my hands with the cold."

Sabrina felt sad and happy all at the same time. Disappointed in herself for ever doubting Harvey, and happy that he was so—so *Harvey-ish.* She threw her arms around him. "Thank you."

Harvey hugged her back. "You don't even know what it is."

"It doesn't matter," Sabrina said. "I'll love it."

"Open it anyway."

Sabrina did, pulling the paper away to reveal a heart-shaped bracelet with double bands and a tiny diamond centered on each band. "Oh, Harvey, it's beautiful."

"It doesn't really have the hand-crafted look of that bracelet you were wearing earlier this week," Harvey said. "But I thought you'd like it."

"I do." And suddenly Sabrina knew exactly what she wanted to get Harvey in addition to the candy heart she had left at the Spellman house. She pointed it into her pocket, then took it out and handed it to him. "I've got something for you. Open it."

Harvey did, and found the ugliest porcelain pig Sabrina had ever seen in the Other Realm in Edna's What(?)Not Shoppe. It fit comfortably into Harvey's hand, pale pink and spotted with red hearts. The huge ears were also heart-shaped, flaring and broad.

"I wanted to get it for you because of that dream you told me about," Sabrina said. "Just to let you know that if you ever really did get captured by a witch and turned into a pig, I'd come after you. I wanted you to have a reminder of that."

"Sab," Harvey said, taking her into his arms, "I've never doubted you."

"Just see that you never do, Harvey Kinkle."

[illegible] Harvey said, [illegible]

[illegible]

[illegible]

"[illegible]," Harvey said, [illegible]
I've never doubted you."

[illegible]

About the Author

Mel Odom believes in magic and considers himself lucky because magic believes in him too. Otherwise, how could he ever have gotten the chance to share all of Sabrina's adventures with the readers?

He lives in Moore, Oklahoma, with his wife and five kids, and finds only the best kind of magic that having a family can bring. Little miracles happen every day, especially with the new baby in the house. And he believes in the supernatural as well, because he shares that house with a poltergeist named Not Me. Because every time something gets mysteriously broken or something is suspiciously left undone, his children point out that it was Not Me.

Author of two other Sabrina books, *Sabrina Goes to Rome* and *Harvest Moon,* he's also written for the series *The Secret World of Alex Mack* and *The Journey of Allen Strange.* He's also written books in SF, suspense, fantasy, adventure, and game-related fields.

Through the magic of the Internet, interested readers can find him at: denimbyte@aol.com